GUN LUCK

The killer left no trail as he roamed the range, gunning down farmers, burning their homes. The prime suspect was Ike Savage, whose cattle empire was overrun by nesters. But Savage proved his innocence by hiring Parker, a roving gambler, as fast with guns as he was with dice, to trap the killer.

GUN LUCK

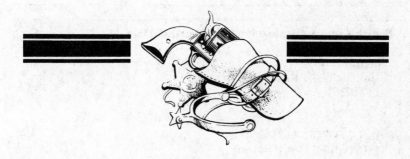

Lee Floren

ATLANTIC LARGE PRINT
Chivers Press, Bath, England.
Curley Publishing, Inc.,
South Yarmouth, Mass., USA.

Library of Congress Cataloging-in-Publication Data

Floren, Lee.
  Gun luck / Lee Floren.
      p.   cm.—(Atlantic large print)
    ISBN 0–7927–0057–0 (lg. print)
    1. Large type books.   I. Title.
  [PS3511.L697G84 1990]   89–17016
  813′.52—dc20   CIP

British Library Cataloguing in Publication Data

Floren, Lee *1910–*
  Gun luck.—(Atlantic large print)
  I. Title
  813′.52 [F]

  ISBN 0–7451–9633–0
  ISBN 0–7451–9645–4 pbk

This Large Print edition is published by Chivers Press, England, and
Curley Publishing, Inc, U.S.A. 1990

Published by arrangement with Donald MacCampbell, Inc

U.K. Hardback ISBN 0 7451 9633 0
U.K. Softback ISBN 0 7451 9645 4
U.S.A. Softback ISBN 0 7927 0057 0

Copyright 1954 by Arcadia House

GUN LUCK

CHAPTER ONE

First, Parker heard the shot. He pulled his bay back into the snow-covered buckbrush; he listened, a big man, heavy with his sheepskin overcoat. There was no more shooting; just that one shot. He knew something about guns; that had been a pistol report, probably a .45.

He felt tense, tight in leather. One shot, somewhere out there in the snow—out there in the falling snow that cut his vision to a few feet. When he had left Circle that morning, the April sky had been clear with spring. The wind had hit him in the badlands, and when he had started down into Muleshoe Valley it was thick with snow. A freak late spring snowstorm.

Parker listened.

How far away had the shot been? That was hard to tell, with snow falling to muffle the sound's passage. Maybe a quarter-mile, maybe half. Probably some farmer out shooting jackrabbits. He put his spurs softly to his bay, and the animal moved ahead ten feet. Suddenly Parker pulled him back into the covering buckbrush.

A rider drifted by, then. He rode fast, pushing through the storm—a grey, snow-shrouded figure, pulling on his right

1

mitten. Parker got the swift impression that the mitten had been taken off so the man—whoever he was—could handle a gun with his right hand.

The storm swallowed him.

Parker stirred, cold biting his legs despite his angora chaps. He would not know that rider if he saw him again, but he would recognize the horse—a heavy-legged, thick-shouldered grey gelding marked by dark splotches across his wide rump. Parker put the picture of that horse inside him, stored it for future reference.

He came out of the brush, rode north toward Elkhorn. He was in a fenced lane. He saw a fire to the east, then. A farmhouse was burning, bright in the snowstorm. Parker looked at the burning house, then back at the rider whom he had glimpsed. He shrugged his thin shoulders, and his darkly handsome face showed no interest.

None of my business, he thought.

He started to ride past, then stopped.

He turned his horse and rode through the open gate; he glanced down, noticing that a horse had recently drifted out of this gate. The house was burning rapidly, as if it had been sprayed at the base with kerosene; flames were eating up the dried siding and the roof was sagging.

Parker saw the legs of a man sticking out of the door. He left his horse, pulled his

2

sheepskin coat's collar up around his face, and ran to the house. The heat beat against his unprotected forehead. He got the legs and pulled the man out, dragging him through the loose snow. He rubbed his own forehead with cold snow and drove the heat out of his skin.

Kneeling, he looked at the man—dead as he had suspected. He was a heavy-set, blocky man of about Parker's age, twenty-five. Fire had eaten slightly into his flannel shirt and woolen pants and his shoes were heavy brogans. He was a farmer, Parker saw, and he had a bullet through his head.

Parker remembered the shot and the strange rider. He got to his feet and rubbed his hands on his chaps before putting on his mittens. This was no business of his.

He got his saddle and rode out.

*　　*　　*

Thirty minutes later, he came to the ledge. The snow had fallen back, its freaky fury spent against man, animal, and nature; Muleshoe Valley lay below him, to his left and right. Parker studied it, shifted in saddle. Beyond this valley lay another range of hills; beyond those hills were the Milk River Valley and more hills; and beyond these last hills were the scrub-pined slopes of Wood Mountain, up in Canada. Parker was going to Canada.

3

Elkhorn town was straight ahead, about three miles. He looked back. The fire had finally died. He looked at his watch. It was ten minutes to one, and he was hungry; Elkhorn would do for a meal.

Parker single-footed the bay down the main street. A small town with one block of business houses—most of these being saloons—and two stores. There was a lumberyard at the outskirts. He glanced at the fresh lumber and remembered that somewhere he had heard that farmers were moving into Muleshoe. He remembered also the shacks he had seen back on the edge of the valley, and the burning house.

A sign said, Sheriff's Office, and Parker glanced at it, dismissed it. He saw another sign, The Elkhorn Café; that had more appeal. He put the bay to its hitchrack and went inside, nodding to the girl behind the counter.

He said, 'I'd like a steak, miss, with spuds and the rest. I'm going to put my horse in the livery, and I'll be right back.' He laid a silver dollar on the counter.

She smiled and said, 'You keep that, mister, until you okay the meal.'

Parker said, 'I'll be back,' and looked at her for a long moment. She was tall and wiry, but she was not slim. Her hair was brown, her eyes too.

Parker said, 'I'll be back,' and added,

4

'pronto.'

He turned to leave.

A man's voice said harshly, 'Wait a minute fellow'; Parker stopped and turned. The man got out of a booth at the far end of the café, where he and another man had been drinking coffee. He was short, and hours in the saddle had warped his thick legs to the barrel of a horse.

'You're new here, ain't you?' the man asked.

Parker looked at him. 'I just rode in,' he said. After a while he added, 'Why?'

The thick jowls grew red. Parker saw this man was quick-tempered. 'What's your job here in Elkhorn, fellow?'

Parker felt the stirrings of anger. 'I told you I'm just riding through. Or if I didn't make it plain enough, I implied it. Can't you understand language the way I speak it?'

The girl said hurriedly, 'Please, men, please.'

Parker spoke to her. 'There'll be no trouble, miss. Not from me, at least.' He turned again to go. And again the man's voice stopped him. 'Just make sure you're not a farmer who aims to settle here, mister, 'cause if you are we'll make it hot for you.'

Parker remembered the fire, remembered the man he had dragged out—the man who had been shot and killed, then evidently pushed into the flames. Somebody had made

5

it hot for him . . . and he had been a farmer.

'So you make it hot,' he said, 'for the farmers?'

The short man peered at him sharply, and the lanky man got out of the booth, uncoiling his great slim length. He had a long thin nose and a long pointed jaw; there was a deceptive slowness about him.

Parker marked him as dangerous.

The slim man asked, 'What way did you ride into town?'

Parker lied, 'From the east, from Saco.'

The slim man sat down again, ran his empty coffee cup around on the oilcloth, seemingly dismissing Parker. The thick man looked hard at Parker and sat down, too. Parker smiled a little with his lips only.

'Is the jury pleased with my answers?'

The thin man shrugged. The thick fellow nodded a little. Parker looked at the girl, and noticed the fear had left her brown eyes. This puzzled him a little. Evidently these men were cowmen and they didn't want more farmers moving in on their range. And they had figured him as a hoeman so had warned him ahead of time. Was that it?

★　　　★　　　★

He got his horse and walked toward the livery leading the animal. The sun was warm and the snow was changing into water. Well,

6

there was some good to this late freak storm—the grass and grain would get some moisture and both would need it, for the average Montana summer was dry and hot.

'Come here, sir,' a voice said.

Parker halted, looking around. The sheriff sat inside his office on a swivel chair, and the office door was open. Parker asked, 'Did you call me, sir?'

'I'd like to talk to you.'

Parker let his reins drop and came inside the small office. There were chairs and a roll-top desk against the far wall. He was slender, this man, and around fifty; wind and storm had marked his long face, drawing fine wrinkles across it. Parker saw something else on that face, and he wondered if it were pain.

Parker said, 'Well, sir?'

Dull blue eyes studied him from under straw-colored eyebrows. 'You're no farmer,' the sheriff said. 'You're either a bartender or a gambler. Could I see your hands?'

Parker smiled. 'No use. I'm a gambler.'

'There's a living for a square gambler here.'

'Some claim there is no such animal.'

'Such as what?'

'A square gambler.'

The sheriff started coughing into a blue bandanna. Parker waited respectfully for the spasm to pass. He saw a letter on the desk, addressed in bold handwriting to Sheriff Ed Jones, Elkhorn, Montana. Again, he

7

remembered the fire, the dead man. Should he tell the sheriff about this?

He decided against it.

'You were in the café,' the sheriff said. 'That girl in there is Millie Williams, and she's single. Can you imagine that, fellow? A girl that's pretty and still single at twenty-three?'

'She might be particular.'

Parker wondered where this conversation was leading.

'You come the south road?'

Parker fabricated again. 'No, from the east. From Saco.'

Sheriff Ed Jones coughed again. 'Day by day, the bugs get deeper. Should go to Arizona—or New Mex—like the quacks say. But what the devil, I've seen my share of it. I was through the Wire Cutter's War in Wyomin'; I've had a few dance hall girls on my knees. Look at the little filly there, now. Cute as a bug nuzzlin' under a Navaho rug.'

Parker looked.

'Who is she?'

'Jetta Savage. She's single, too. Twenty, I'd say. Red hair and grey eyes. What a mixture!'

She was short, not over five feet. Her grey beaver stetson had a braided chin strap and red hair peeped from under it. Her riding skirt and jacket were of buckskin and had porcupine quills for markings. Under the jacket was a silk blouse.

'She's got a sister, too. Older than Jetta.'

Parker's glance met Jetta Savage's. Then she looked past him and spoke to Sheriff Ed Jones. Jones lifted a hand in reply, and the girl went into the Elkhorn Café.

'Daughters of a cowman?' asked Parker.

'Yeah, ol' Ike Savage. Ike's on his back now—dying inch by inch, day by day. Horse busted his back some two years ago. The other girl is different. Ah, she's a fine woman, is Connie Savage.'

Parker smiled, 'Is she married?'

'No. She's twenty-two, I guess.' Ed Jones's eyes were tired. 'What difference does it make to you, friend? You're ridin' through.'

Was there a threat in his voice?

Parker lifted his thin shoulders. 'Just a question, Jones.' Then he stood there, watching a man ride into town. He was astraddle an old mare that had collar marks on her bony shoulders. He rode bareback despite the razor-edge backbone of the beast. He left the horse and came inside.

'Luke Smith's cabin burned, Sheriff! I just came from there. Saw the flames from my place and went over there, but I was too late. I rode from there straight into town.'

Ed Jones looked at this new man.

Parker was silent.

'Where's Luke Smith?' asked the sheriff.

'Dead! I found him in the snow. Some of

his clothes were burnt.' The farmer caught his breath. 'Somebody's shot Luke through the brains!'

CHAPTER TWO

Parker took his bay to the livery. The stable-man was a dour, aged individual with seamy eyes. He looked at the sack tied across the pack of Parker's saddle. Parker untied it and tossed him the half-filled quart of bourbon.

'You got good eyes,' he said.

The ancient drank. 'And an appetite to go with the eyes.' He uncorked the bottle and sighed loudly. 'Good stuff.' He made no move to hand back the bottle.

'Keep it,' said Parker.

'Thanks.'

Parker stripped the bay, hung up his saddle and bridle and looked at his saddlebags for a long moment. The bay went to work on a manger of blue-joint hay and a bin of ground oats.

Sheriff Ed Jones entered, the farmer with him. The hostler put down his bottle and led them back into the barn. Parker went outside and stood in the brilliant spring sunshine.

The two men he had met in the café came up. 'What's going on?' asked the short one.

'Where's the sheriff and that farmer going?'

'Why ask me?'

The tall man said, 'Don't get huffy, stranger.'

Parker smiled. He went down the street. Jetta Savage came out of a store. She said, 'Are you a farmer here, stranger?'

Parker looked at her with lazy indifference. 'That question has been asked of me before in this town,' he said. 'My answer is the same: no.' He let a smile pull at his thin lips, yet his eyes measured her.

'Oh,' she said.

Parker said, 'And if I were a farmer, what difference would it make to you?' He pretended he did not know she was Ike Savage's daughter.

'I'm Jetta Savage,' she said. 'We don't like farmers, we Savages don't. You see, we run the big outfit around this valley, the Heart Bar Six. Farmers and cattle don't get along.'

Parker's eyes were flat on her. 'You look like you wouldn't be hard to get along with,' he murmured.

She was angry. 'Move on, you saddle bum.'

'You stopped me,' said Parker sharply.

Her grey eyes were sharp with quick lights. She let this emotion pass, and she smiled, and the smile was warm.

Parker murmured, 'You're prettier that way,' and left her.

11

There was something wrong with this town, and with this range.

Parker thought, I'll eat and get out of this Elkhorn town, or they'll pull me into this mess. And I don't want that.

Millie Williams said, 'Your order is ready, sir.'

Parker sat on a stool. This was the slack hour and he was the only customer. Back in the kitchen, the cook clattered with a pot and lid. He cursed in a dull monotone. 'Jack,' called the girl, 'stop that swearing.'

She went to the register and started checking.

Parker ate slowly, enjoying the well-cooked meal. The coffee was good—just right, the way he liked it. Millie finished her work and came back from the kitchen. She refilled his coffee cup.

*   *   *

'Would you talk to me?' asked Parker.

Her eyes were level. 'You're a pretty good-looking man; yes, I guess so.' She smiled. 'Lonesome?'

'Who were those two men in here? Those two who talked to me just a while ago?' He looked out the window. 'There they ride now.'

The short man rode a pinto stud, a high animal who tossed his head against the bit.

12

The tall man rode a heavy black, a sure-footed horse.

'The man on the pinto is Kirt Stanton. He's ramrod for old Ike Savage's Heart Bar Six iron. Savage is in bed, you know; broken back or something. That was his daughter who talked to you.'

'And the other man?'

'He's the banker, Martin Trundell.'

Parker nodded over his coffee cup. The pair stopped in front of the bank, where Trundell ran inside. He came out carrying a rifle and they rode on again, heading south at a long slope.

'Trundell doesn't look like a banker to me,' murmured Parker.

'He's been here two years, I guess. He bought the bank from old Matthew Harry. He knows his banks, I guess. I wonder where they are going?'

Parker told her he had heard that a man named Luke Smith was dead. He told her he had been in Sheriff Jones's office when a farmer had brought in the news.

'Smith was a nice fellow,' she said. 'He had a wife and child back east, I believe.' She did not seem concerned.

'This happen before?'

'No, nothing this bad. Of course, there have been some clashes between Savage riders and farmers, but only fist fights so far.'

'You don't seem concerned.'

She shrugged. 'Why should I be? Of course, indirectly it concerns me, but—this has been building up for some time, some months. It'll come to a head now, of course, and there'll be gunplay.'

'Who'll win?'

'The farmers, of course. No, they're not gunmen, that's true. But if they kill one off, another will come and take his place. And the killing won't go on long . . . if it does start. The governor will send in the state militia, I guess.'

'What does Savage think of it?'

She rubbed the counter with a damp rag. 'Look, mister, you're flat on your back, we'll say. You're old and sick and you got two hellions for daughters. Your wife has been dead for years and you've fought blizzards and Indians and raised two wildcats. What can you think, when death sits around the corner of each day waiting for you?'

Parker was silent.

She said, 'I didn't see the sheriff ride by.'

'Neither did I.'

'He must've swung around town and rode out through an alley.'

*   *   *

Parker finished his meal in silence. He was killing his last cup of coffee when somebody entered. He did not look at the door. There

14

was a mirror behind the counter and he glanced into it.

A woman. She wore levis, a flannel shirt, a calfskin coat that was marked by brush. Her justins were brush-scarred, too, and her spurs chimed with Mexican pesos in the shanks.

Her stetson was lying against her back, the chin strap holding it. Parker saw jet-black hair that was pulled back. It glistened. Her face was round, a little too full, and the lips were a trifle thick. Yet there was a harsh, strong beauty in that overmature face.

'Coffee, Millie.'

Parker noticed that Millie only nodded.

'Have you seen that sister of mine?'

Millie said, 'She went into the Mercantile a few minutes ago.'

The girl looked at Parker. 'I'm Connie Savage,' she said.

Parker told her his name. Millie went back into the kitchen. 'The old man wanted me to come in and keep an eye on that angel sister of mine for him. Why, I don't know. When you get old, you have whims, I guess.'

'I guess so.'

'You're new to the basin, aren't you?'

'Just rode in.'

'You looking for work?'

Parker smiled. 'I've spent a lifetime running away from it,' he said. 'Yes, I'm looking for it . . . so that I know where it is and it won't get me unawares. A man always

15

has to know where his enemies are, you know.'

The hard line ran across her full mouth. 'Does that go for a woman, too?'

'Yes, I'd say so.'

'Maybe,' she said. 'I don't know who my enemies are. Maybe I'm my biggest enemy.' She laughed slightly at that.

Parker was silent.

She spoke finally. 'I thought maybe you wanted a job on the Heart Bar Six. Of course, I thought you weren't a saddle man, but I thought I'd ask to make sure.'

'You don't want rope men,' said Parker slowly.

She stabbed a quick look at him.

'You want gunmen,' he added.

'I saw you ride in,' she said. 'You came from the south. I was on the rimrock, and that freak storm caught me, and I saw you come off the hills.'

Parker remembered suddenly he had told the sheriff and Kirt Stanton and Martin Trundell that he had come over from Saco. What was this filly doing back in the hills? Had she seen the fire at Luke Smith's place, and did she know Luke Smith was dead, evidently murdered?

'You saw somebody else,' he said. 'I came over from Saco.'

She said very softly, 'Don't call me a liar, mister,' and her eyes held some strange

16

promise, a sudden softness. 'My eyes are good.'

'Your eyes,' stated Parker bluntly, 'are the eyes of a woman, that's all.' He got to his feet.

Her fingers touched him lightly on the sleeve. 'Don't make a mistake,' she said. 'Don't stay on this range.'

He was silent for a second. 'But you wanted to hire me.'

Her shoulders lifted, fell. 'If you went to work for the Heart Bar Six, you'd be all right. But, fellow, I think you saw—' She fell silent. 'Just move on, and we'll see you get out of the basin.'

Parker said cynically, 'And you'll escort me out, I suppose?'

'I'll hold your soft hand,' she murmured ironically.

★   ★   ★

Parker went to the barn. The afternoon sun was warm; steam lifted from the earth. A dog was digging out a gopher. Parker glanced at him and said, 'You've got a long chore ahead, pooch,' and entered the livery.

The hostler sat on a bench, shaggy head on his chest. Parker caught a sharp odor of whisky and saw that the bottle was empty beside the old man. He went to his horse and saddled him.

17

Somebody had gone through his saddlebags.

He was sure of that. He had had their contents arranged neatly; now they were jumbled up, bulky. Had Sheriff Ed Jones done that? Or had Kirt Stanton and Martin Trundell searched his belongings? And why?

He went through the bags, working slowly. Nothing was missing. He left the horse in the stall and walked to the door. Three riders were coming into Elkhorn. They led a horse that carried a dead man jackknife across its saddle.

Luke Smith . . .

Parker looked at Stanton and Trundell. Then he looked at Sheriff Ed Jones. He looked hard and long at the lawman's horse. He had seen that horse before this day. The horse was a big grey and he had hard, dark marks across his rump.

CHAPTER THREE

Parker thought, One of those deals, huh? and he went back and unsaddled his own horse. When he got to the sheriff's office the three were untying the dead man with a troup of townsmen around them. Parker noticed that very little was said by anybody.

'You still in town?' a woman's voice asked.

Connie Savage sat on the buggy seat, reins in her hand. Jetta sat beside her, and Parker saw she was a little drunk. Jetta's horse was tied behind the rig. Parker smiled a little.

'I stayed because I wanted to see you again,' he said smoothly.

Connie turned the buggy. Jetta said, 'All right, guardian angel, let's get these hay-burners running, huh?'

Mud was flung by the buggy's wheels.

A townsman smiled a little.

Jones and Stanton carried the dead man into the office, with Trundell following them. Jones said, 'Trundell, go down and get the coroner.'

Trundell looked at Parker, then went down the street.

Parker turned away. He went to the hotel where he registered, got an upstairs room where he could look out on the main street. Below him stood the horses and people in front of the sheriff's office. Opposite the hotel was a vacant lot. Parker pulled the wrinkled blind down to the sill and hooked it over the nail. He jacked a chair under the door knob, after locking it and leaving the key in the slot.

He slept until it was dark.

Once he heard somebody out in the hall. For years he had slept during the daytime, getting up in the late afternoon. He had slept in rooms over saloons, in hotels, in private homes, in barns. He had slept in tents, in

19

tepees. He shaved and washed well, rubbing his face hard with the rough towel. He ate at the Elkhorn Café. Millie Williams was back in the kitchen, cooking. Another girl was waiting on the counter.

Millie walked by.

Parker said, 'You changed jobs, huh?'

'The cook,' she said. She added, 'He took that extra drink—that one too many.' She was tired; her face showed it. Parker saw that it was an honest tiredness, one brought by hard clean work.

He paid and went into the moist spring night. Darkness was thick, and he went to the livery barn. The old man still slept, only this time he lay on the floor snoring loudly, his mouth open.

Parker got his bay and rode west.

*   *   *

He rode at a long lope, covered the fifteen miles in a short time, it seemed. The bay was fresh from his afternoon rest. Parker left him at the corral, tying him in the darkness.

The house was big, stuck wth gables. Parker looked at it, noticed the lamplight from the side room. The bunkhouse had lights but no persons stirred at the ranch. No dogs barked, either. He wondered about that; usually a ranch had a dog or two about it.

He went to the house and knocked. He got

no answer except the dull hollow boom through the building. He knocked again. This brought an old man, a bent-over gnome who came out of the shadows of the living-room and opened the door a little.

'Who are you?' he asked.

He was an Indian, Parker saw. Probably a Sioux. He was ageless, and his eyes were sharp and dark as the eyes of a rat. He looked like a rat, too, bent over that way by Time's push.

'I'm Parker. I want to see Ike Savage.'

A short pause. Then in broken English, 'Savage is sick. He sees nobody. See one of his girls, his daughters.'

'Where are they?'

'They have cabins. That way.' He jerked a thumb west.

Parker remembered the cabins. There had been lights in them. 'Savage is expecting me. He sent for me.'

'He sent for nobody.'

Parker pushed the door open and went inside. The old buck had his hand on his belt and Parker saw the bone-handled knife there.

'Who's there, Crazy Springs?'

'Strange man, Ike. Name Parker.'

'For Pete's sake, don't stand there and argue! Let him come in.'

Crazy Springs stepped back. 'He's this way,' he said. He led Parker down a hall. The door was open and a lamp burned low inside.

It glowed in the rat-like eyes in the parchment skin.

Parker went alone into the room. Books lined all the walls and the dim lamplight showed on dark bindings. The room was small. Parker caught a dense, cloying odor, almost nauseating. It was the smell of fresh lupine from the many vases. Parker wondered how the man stood the odor.

Then he looked at Ike Savage.

The man was only a shell. There was life in him, for his lips moved as he talked, and now and then his eyes rolled a little in sunken sockets. One hand lay over the sheet, and Parker saw that it was emaciated, almost a claw. The cheeks had sunk back, letting the cheekbones lift, and the eyebrows were thin like the man's hair, grey and wasted. Parker caught the grim impression that this man was alive, yet he was dead.

Savage's voice was a husky whisper. 'Stare if you want to, sir. Perhaps you find a grim pleasure in it.'

Parker said, 'I'm sorry.'

'Sorry for what, sir? Sorry because you're looking at a man who'll soon know the answer to the great riddle? Sorry because I am doomed to die soon?'

'We're all under that sentence,' murmured Parker.

'Sit down,' said Ike Savage. He coughed. 'What do you want, sir?'

Parker was quiet for some time. Savage's eyes were fierce on him. Parker got to his feet and walked quietly to the door. Crazy Springs sat outside.

Parker said, 'Leave us alone, please.'

'What boss say?'

'Get out,' ordered Savage.

Parker watched the buck walk down the hall and enter the big living-room. He went to the window, glanced out and came back. 'You sent for somebody to ride into Muleshoe?' he said.

'What are you talking about?'

Parker sat down again. 'They went through my saddlebags. Who, I don't know. Might have been the sheriff or it might have been your range boss, Kirt Stanton. Or it might have been your banker down in town, this Trundell gent.'

'Talk more,' said Savage.

'They were looking for somebody to ride in; they thought I was somebody else. They wanted to make sure, and they thought I might have something to identify me in my bags.' He added, 'They were wrong.'

'Who are you?'

'I'm a gambler. Name of Parker.'

'Given name?'

'Had one, I guess. Maybe I lost it. Does it matter?'

Ike Savage breathed deeply. The covers rose a little over his scrawny chest. 'I have

23

pain,' he said. 'I have it all the time. So does Ed Jones. I'd like to outlive that whelp, though.'

Parker waited. The night was heavy. The lupine scent was heavy, too. He wanted to get out.

'You're smart,' said Savage.

'I hope so. If I'm not, I'll be dead soon, I figure.'

'So your breath is at stake? You want to keep on breathing, is that it?'

'Yes, that's it.'

'Explain yourself.'

Parker spoke quietly. 'They think I'm a man you sent for, I take it. Every move I make is watched. They searched my saddlebags; they tried the door to my room. I want to get out of this basin in one piece. I have nothing at stake here. I want you to call off your wolves. I want you to pass the word out that I'm just a plain, everyday gambler—not the man you sent for.'

'You think I have that power?'

'I do.'

Savage lay hard against his pillow. He closed his eyes. He seemed to cease breathing. Then he spoke again.

'I haven't that power.'

Parker got to his feet. 'Then I'll gun my way out,' he said. 'I didn't want to do that, either. I might get killed, and I want to live.' He spoke simply and to the point. 'But I thought maybe you had sent for a man.'

'I did, once. That man got killed, I hear.'

Parker studied him. 'Luke Smith?'

'That's right.'

Parker asked, 'Then who's behind this, Savage? Who's fighting these farmers, if it ain't you and your Heart Bar Six? It's valley talk.'

'It's not me, Parker. It might be my daughters; I don't know. But I think there is something bigger behind it. Who, I don't know. Do you?'

'No, I don't.'

'Do you want to find out?'

'Not particularly.'

'There's ten thousand in it,' said Savage.

'I've seen that many times on a table,' said Parker. 'I've flipped one card and lost it. And I've won it, too.'

'Twenty.'

Parker shrugged.

'Thirty.'

'No.'

'Fifty thousand, then?'

Parker asked, 'Where will the money be?'

'In the bank. In Elkhorn.'

Parker thought of Martin Trundell. 'No, in the Saco bank. Why do you want me to stop this trouble?'

'Two women.'

Parker considered that. This man had strong blood, and it was their blood. They

25

were strong and tough, then, too. But strength had to be directed into channels, or else it was destructive. Theirs was in the wrong channels.

But he couldn't tell him that.

'I want this ranch for them,' said Savage.

'You can't hold it,' said Parker quietly. 'Farmers will come in more and more—this bottom land will be wheat and alfalfa and fences. I saw it happen when irrigation hit the Gila bottom out of Yuma. I've seen it other places, too.'

'I don't expect to hold the bottom land,' said Savage slowly. 'I ordered Stanton to pull back into the hills. I can buy hay from the farmers cheaper than my crews used to cut wild bluejoint on the valley. And this is better hay, too—alfalfa hay. Stanton told me he'd pull cattle back.'

Parker stood straight. 'So the deal is this, huh? You want to find out who is causing this trouble. You sent Luke Smith to find out. He came in as a farmer; they got wise—killed him.'

Savage looked at him fiercely and nodded. 'Why?'

Savage gestured with a claw. 'Look, man, look. You're old, and your back is broke. All your life, you've been proud of yourself, of your destiny. Savage, Savage. That's a good name, Parker.' He added, 'It was a good name.'

Parker saw his fierce pride.

'You'll keep this to yourself,' said Parker.

'I'm no fool.'

Parker bowed slightly. '*Adios, señor.*' He went out into the hall. Crazy Springs sat at the kitchen table playing solitaire. Parker looked at him.

'Why were you trying to eavesdrop?'

The buck's eyes were without thoughts. 'No know what you say.'

'Why were you listening?'

The grizzled head nodded, the greasy braids moving. 'They maybe kill him. Send man to kill him.'

'Who's they?'

The buck shrugged. 'Me no know.'

Parker went outside. He stood for a minute or two on the long, dark porch and rolled a slow cigarette.

CHAPTER FOUR

Jetta Savage let ten minutes run by. She came out of the shadows beside the barn and went to a cabin below the horse corrals. There was a light in the cabin, and she knocked softly.

'Who's there?' asked Kirt Stanton.

'Me, Jetta.'

Stanton opened the door. He had a coffee pot bubbling on the wood stove and he put out another cup. Jetta sat down and watched him.

'A social call, Jetta?'

'What else would it be?' she snapped.

Stanton looked at her. 'One lump or two, you bitter-mouthed chicken?' He had irony in his voice.

'None.'

Stanton poured one cup and sat down, Jetta got to her feet and walked to the wall and looked at a picture there that had been cut from a gaudy calendar distributed to saloons. Stanton looked at her pretty back. But when she turned around his eyes were on his coffee cup.

'Well?' she asked.

'You came here,' he said. 'I didn't come looking for you.'

'Parker was here,' she said. 'He saw Dad; they talked. Crazy Springs says he tried to listen; Parker told him to get away. The Indian doesn't know what they were talking about.'

Stanton nodded and sipped noisily.

'You don't seem worried,' she said.

Stanton assured her he was not worried. He had seen Parker's horse when he had ridden in. Maybe Parker had just ridden out to pay a social call. Jetta smiled at that; she reminded the range boss that Parker had not known Ike Savage before, and that Parker had ridden to the Heart Bar Six for a reason.

Stanton lifted his shoulders, let them fall. 'Now beat it,' he said. 'I want to go to bed.'

Jetta said, 'Damn you,' and left.

Outside, she stood silent and thoughtful, looking at Connie's cabin.

She went to the barn and saddled a sorrel horse, led the animal along the edge of the creek, muffling his hoofs on the grass. A quarter-mile from the house she got her saddle and rode toward Elkhorn. The town was dark and silent when she came in. She did not ride to the livery. She left her horse in the brush and walked into town some two hundred yards or so.

The old hostler was asleep in his office, sprawled on the floor with the lamp wicked low. Jetta went down the aisle and stopped and looked for a long second at Parker's horse that was munching hay at the manger. She went out the back door.

There was a light in Sheriff Ed Jones' office. She knocked and came in, and Jones turned his chair and looked at her with surprise in his eyes. He coughed and leaned forward and held his bandanna over his mouth.

'What you doin' in town at this hour?'

'Parker was out to the Heart Bar Six; he talked with Ike Savage. Who is this fellow Parker, Sheriff?'

Jones' eyes were bright. 'Why not ask him? You might find out something then. I don't know anything. Why do you ask?'

'Why do I ask? Use your head, Jones. This thing is getting hot. Luke Smith lies down the street, a bullet hole through his head. The farmers here think a Heart Bar Six man did it. I know none of them did, but the farmers don't know that. It would be an easy thing to hire a man to murder Ike Savage.'

Jones' eyes shifted, held. 'You talk like a fool,' he said.

'It's been done; it could be done.'

Jones rolled an imaginary object between thumb and forefinger. He looked at her for a long time. 'You're a lovely woman, Jetta. But you're a hellcat. Lord help the man—'

'—the man I marry,' she finished. 'You've said that before.'

Jones flushed. 'I'll look into Parker,' he said. He turned back to his desk. She had ceased to exist, as far as he was concerned.

★   ★   ★

She went outside and to the hotel. She spun the register and looked at the number of Parker's room. She started up the stairs, stopped, came down, and went outside again. The town was quiet. She stood on the hotel porch in the shadows. Ed Jones came out of his office, locked it behind him, and went down the street. He cut across an alley and disappeared.

Going home, she thought.

A dog barked.

She went down the street again and came to the back of the bank. Here was a small house of three or four rooms. There was a light inside. She tried the door knob but it was locked, so she knocked softly. Three short knocks and two long knocks. The door opened and she went inside.

Martin Trundell wore a silk dressing-robe over his pajamas and his feet were encased in kidskin slippers. But if he was surprised at her late visit his thin face did not show it.

'Sit down, Jetta.'

She took a chair. He went to the sideboard and got glasses and a whisky bottle. 'Or would you rather have something else besides whisky?'

'Whisky's all right.'

He sat down, crossed his knees, adjusted his robe, and looked at his whisky. 'To Muleshoe,' he said, and drank.

She drank, too.

'Well, Jetta?'

'I just came from the ranch,' she said. 'Parker was out there this evening. He was talking with Ike Savage. No, I don't know what they said. Parker shooed Crazy Springs away and kept one eye out of the window to see nobody was listening there. I wish I knew what they talked about.'

Trundell poured another drink. He looked

inquiringly at her, and Jetta shook her head. 'Have you told this to Stanton?'

'I have. He didn't say much.'

'What is your plan, Jetta?'

'I think Ike Savage hired him. He wants to find out who murdered Luke Smith. He doesn't know that I know about those late night visits that Smith paid to the Heart Bar Six.'

Trundell nodded. 'We'll find out something,' he said. 'You better go home and go to bed.'

Jetta got. her horse and rode south. The moonlight was golden now: it was sombre and wise, lying close to the earth. She rode through it, and the moon heeled over and started its fall. She rode for an hour. The end of that hour found her deep in the south hills, thick in the folds of the benches and mesas. She followed a wagon road for a while; then she left this and followed a dim buffalo trail that played out, and she rode across the country, bullberry and choke-cherry trees dark and wavering in the light. She went around the toe of a hill and rode into the buckbrush.

She pushed open the plank door of a one-room sod shack and went into the darkness. She crossed the dark strip—she seemed familiar with it—and there was another door against a cave set in the hillside. This was locked, and she knocked on it.

But the voice came from the darkness behind her. 'Who is there?'

She turned, startled, and said, 'Jetta, Jetta.'

'What are you doing here at this hour of the night?'

Her eyes were becoming accustomed to the darkness. She made out the man's indefinite form: he was stooped, bent over.

'Let's talk inside.'

He crossed the strip, walking slowly, and he opened the door. They went into the hill, into a large room with a lamp lit in it. This cavern had been carved out of the hill with a shovel and a pick. Cottonwood supports ran upright and the ceiling was finished in rough-sawed pine. The walls were finished, too, and here and there were windows, which in reality led to twisted air shafts for ventilation.

*   *   *

The man was old, his beard grey and scraggly. His clothes were dirty and they hung sack-like to his shrunken, stooped frame. He had been a big man once with much flesh, but that flesh had fallen away, and now only his bones were big.

Jetta walked to the far end of the room and stopped and looked at an oil painting on the easel. The painting was almost complete.

There was a wildness about the desolate badland scene painted on the tight canvas, and Jetta felt its impact.

'You are just finishing that, André?'

'Yes, soon it will be done.'

She looked at his hands, at the oilpaint that clung to his stubby fingers. 'You have captured the feeling, the emotion of it,' she said. She looked at it again. He watched the hardness leave her thin face, drop from her lips. She was girlish, without veneer, and he decided he liked her better that way.

'I am an old man,' he said. 'Surely a girl of your beauty could find a young man to keep awake at nights.'

She took the hint. She told him about Parker and Ike Savage, and that Parker slept now, down in Elkhorn.

'I do not know this Parker.'

'He's new.' She bit her lip. 'And he's dangerous, I think. He said he came from Saco, but he didn't. He came from the south, during the freak snowstorm yesterday noon.'

'Why did he lie?'

'Why do you think he lied?'

André looked at his huge knuckles. 'You think that he was the one who dragged Luke Smith out of the burning building? You know, the way I figured, Smith should've burned.'

'Oh.'

André asked, 'What do you say, girl?'

34

'Parker has to go. Somebody has to kill him.'

André was silent.

CHAPTER FIVE

Parker was eating breakfast alone in a booth in the Elkhorn Café when Connie Savage sat down opposite him.

'You don't mind, sir?'

Parker smiled. 'You're much prettier than that wall,' he said. 'You're up early, Miss Connie.'

She ordered ham and eggs and coffee. 'I always get up early. I've been back in the hills already, looking at the water and grass back there. We're moving cattle back, you know.'

Parker let his eyebrows raise.

'Ike says to let the farmers have the valley,' she continued. 'So we're letting them have it; sensible, too, I say.'

'A range war isn't nice,' murmured Parker.

Millie Williams glanced at them as she went past. Martin Trundell came in, nodded at Parker, spoke to Connie, and sat on a counter stool.

Parker said, 'You'll excuse me?'

Connie nodded. He paid Millie and went outside. The wind was chilly, and he pulled his coat tight around him. Spring was cold on

35

this northern range. He stood and swung his toothpick between his lips. Well, if Stanton was pulling back Heart Bar Six cattle, as Ike Savage had ordered there should be no trouble here.

Parker thought of the fifty thousand that would be in the Saco bank for him, thought of old Ike Savage, of Savage's deformed hands, lying on the covers of the bed. He didn't care much about the money. Of course, fifty thousand was a lot, but he'd won that and lost that, and it had never stayed with him. And this wouldn't, either.

He got his horse and rode south.

The sun was getting warm, and when he reached Smith's homestead, the chilly wind had died down. He left his horse at the gate and walked to the ruins of the ranch building. The ashes were black against the green earth. A pup was whimpering behind a clump of sage-brush. He was just a few months old, and he was hungry. Smith's dog, Parker figured.

There were tracks, yes; too many. Dozens of people had visited these ruins; they had tramped the ground to a muddy pulp, they had thrown cigarette butts around, and they had turned their rigs in front of the foundation. Parker found some blood by the rock foundation where the door had been. Smith's blood.

He looked around some more, then swore

in disgust. He had a hunch every move he made on this range was watched. Maybe eyes were watching him now from some brush-covered hill, eyes using field-glasses. They would be wondering what he—a gambler—was doing at the ruins of a farmer's house.

Parker picked up the whimpering pup. He rode to the closest farmhouse, a mile down the section line. It was a sod shack with a sod barn, and a man got up off the bench beside the door.

'You're Parker, ain't you?' The man didn't wait for an answer. 'I'm Jed Hawkins. I see you down in town yesterday.'

'I rode past Smith's farm,' said Parker, 'found this pup there; guess he belonged to Smith. I thought maybe you'd take care of him.'

'Little Sonny Porter had him in their buggy,' said Hawkins. 'I figured he'd take him home, but the pup must've jumped out an' run back. Yeah, I'll take care of him. Just dump him off.'

Parker leaned on one stirrup and let the pup drop a few feet to the wet soil. He ran into the open door of the shanty, and Jed Hawkins laughed. 'Think's he's home, I reckon. I'd like to have seen what the pup seen yesterday.'

Parker nodded.

'Luke Smith an' me was friends, Parker.

I'd like to line the man on my sights, I tell you. I'm keepin' on the lookout.'

'Savage is moving his cattle back,' said Parker. 'Or so I hear.'

'You stayin' here for a spell?'

'Might line up a table in some saloon,' said Parker. 'This seems to be a pretty good town and there seems to be some loose change. Might stay for a day or two.'

'Might be easy to take over Smith's homestead rights.'

'I'm no farmer.'

'I won't be either unless I can get out to work my ground soon. This danged snowstorm sure jibed the ground up for us farmers. None of us got any too settled nerves, livin' so close to our rifles an' shotguns.'

Parker turned his horse toward Elkhorn. Jetta Savage came down a sidehill, sliding her big horse in the loose earth and mud. Parker pulled in and waited for her to join him, and he lifted his hat a little.

'Riding to town?' asked Jetta.

Parker regarded her with a slow gravity. She was pretty with her red hair and grey eyes, although she had a brassy hardness about her. Again he got the swift impression that her mouth was too hard, and he wondered why.

'Out rescuing dogs,' he said.

She looked at him sharply. 'You seem to do

good at rescue work,' she said.

'What do you mean by that?'

'Oh, nothing.'

'You're ornery,' said Parker. 'Sometimes I think you're mean. I'd hate to be married to a woman like you.'

'You won't be.'

Parker was silent.

'You're not staying in the basin, are you?'

He told her he might run a table in a saloon. She fell silent then, and they rode for a quarter-mile. She turned in leather and opened a saddlebag and brought out a flask. She handed it to him and he uncorked it. He caught the wry flat odor of whisky, handed it back untasted.

'Too early in the morning.'

She drank, corked it, put it away. 'The old man's dying,' she said. 'He lies there, day after day, night after night, hour after hour. He's got the clock close, and he watches that clock and he watches the minutes go. Now and then Crazy Springs moves him in bed.'

'Crazy Springs?'

'He's the old man's Indian. He takes care of the old man. But I thought you knew that.'

'How would I know?' Parker played ignorant.

'Thought maybe somebody had told you in town. There are some sharp tongues down there, and some prying eyes.'

'Your sister told me you were moving your

cattle back.'

'Connie? Where'd you see her?'

Parker told her about meeting Connie at breakfast. Jetta Savage's eyes were bitter suddenly. 'I hate her,' she said. 'I guess you shouldn't hate your flesh and blood, but I do. I hope she never gets in my way. It'll be too bad for her.'

'Why?'

'Is it your business?'

Parker was silent. These sisters were a riddle to him. They were silent the rest of the trip into Elkhorn.

Sheriff Ed Jones stood in front of his office, watching them ride in. They left their broncs in the livery and Jetta went to the café. Jones was sitting down, looking at his boots, when Parker went by. Jones said, 'Sit down, Parker, sit down. Take the load off your boots.'

Parker sat on the bench.

A man went by and said, 'Hello, Jones,' and nodded at Parker, who nodded back. Martin Trundell came out of his bank. He said hello and went into the Fiddleback Saloon. A farmer had his rig in front of the Mercantile. He loaded it with supplies, and then his wife came out and he helped her into the buggy. Jones coughed and spat into the drying earth.

'You were out to Luke Smith's ranch, huh?'

40

Parker thought, Were these the eyes that watched me? and said, 'I rode by, yes. I found Smith's pup and took him over to Jed Hawkins.'

'Did Hawkins keep him?'

Parker said, 'Yes.'

'Hawkins lives close to Smith's place. I questioned him yesterday, but he didn't know anything about Smith's murder. Or maybe Smith wasn't murdered; maybe he killed himself. He was a moody gent, you know. Up one day and down the other.'

'Some are that way,' said Parker. 'I've seen all kinds at the tables.'

He went to the Double Diamond Bar. He had a drink—ice-water and lemon—and got talking with the proprietor. Yes, he could take over a table—might not hit much, and still he might have some luck. Some of the farmers had some money, but most of them were pretty low.

'Your rakeoff?' asked Parker.

'The usual. Ten per cent.'

Parker consented. He had to have some apparent excuse for staying in Elkhorn. He was being watched; he was sure of that when he came into his hotel room at noon. A quick glance showed that everything was as he had left it. Another glance, more slow, showed him a few other things—his razor had been moved a little on the bureau top, his pants hung a little differently in the clothes closet.

41

His warbag and saddlebags had been moved a little beyond the bed-leg.

He went downstairs and asked the clerk if anybody had been in his room. 'Only the maid,' said the clerk.

Parker smiled with a slight twist.

CHAPTER SIX

Parker watched the town from his hotel room window. People moved across it lazily, and he marked their slow courses with great deliberateness.

He heard hoofs.

Sheriff Ed Jones was riding down the main street. Parker watched him pull out of town, his bronc at a long running walk. He saw him go into the folds of the hills toward Smith's farm. Parker sat and looked at the back door of the bank. Twenty minutes later, Martin Trundell came out there and went to the barn behind the building. Three minutes later he led out a saddled black gelding. He turned the oxbow stirrup around and put his boot into it and went up, riding out of town at a long lazy lope.

It took him three minutes to saddle that horse, thought Parker. That means he's used to throwing a saddle on a bronc and finding the cinches.

Parker got to his feet and stretched. He looked longingly at the bed, then went out into the hall. He started to lock the door behind him, then smiled and stuck the key in his vest pocket, leaving the room unlocked. He went down the back stairway into the alley, and he stopped once on his way to the barn. That was at the Fiddleback Saloon where he bought a quart for the old livery hostler.

The aged eyes wrinkled. 'You ride a lot, fellow.' He pushed a grimy thumb toward a big sorrel in the manger. 'Take that bronc, yours is sorta tuckered out.' He broke the seal on the bottle.

When Parker rode out of the barn the old man was admiring the ceiling by looking up over the bottle as the whisky tumbled down his throat.

Parker rode west. He reached the foothills, and these hid him from any eyes watching him from Elkhorn. Now he swung south. The sorrel was a hill horse and tough against the slants for downgrade rides; Parker bunched his shoulder muscles and took the spring.

He was getting higher. Buckbrush was giving way to scrub pine with its gnarled, stunted growth. Parker thought of the gold camps to the west and north: in the Little Rockies around Landusky and Zortman, and up in Canada in the Wood Mountain section.

Tables would be running wild and wide open there, but down in Elkhorn—

He came to a wide mesa on top of the benchland. He left the heaving sorrel with dragging reins and walked to the lip, carrying the field-glasses he had had in his case on the saddle. He settled there in the brush, and the tumbling running vista of Muleshoe Basin lay below and north.

Parker was struck again by the wildness of this northern range. Rolling hills now green with spring grass folded and lifted and fell, then ran out of sight when his vision failed against the distance. There was rim of sky over this, blue and thin and without life; then over this lifted a few clouds, moving across with a high unfelt wind as sheep move before a herder and his dogs.

Parker put the glasses across the land below. He focused them accurately and brought clear lines to shimmery objects. He swept them up trails and across trails, and finally found Sheriff Ed Jones.

Jones still held to a running walk, his grey moving across space. He was about two miles away, riding toward Luke Smith's farm.

Parker found Martin Trundell, too; the banker was between him and Jones, and he was shading Jones. Parker leaned back and put a cigar slowly between his lips. He licked the raw end, getting the taste of tobacco, and he cupped a match and lit it and watched.

What was this, anyway?

★ ★ ★

Jones rode to Jed Hawkins' shack. He stayed there for some twenty minutes, talking to the farmer. Parker could see the pup running and playing with the chickens. Hawkins threw a stick at the dog and made him go into the house.

Trundell sat his horse in some brush above the farmer's homestead, hidden there from any eyes below. Parker knew that if he had not seen the banker ride into the brush, he would never have been able to discern him through his glasses. For the brush was high and thick, and to the casual glance without a horse and rider in it.

He turned on his hips and sent his glasses across the rim of the hills behind him, wondering if any eyes were watching him. He studied the terrain closely, moving the glasses slowly, and he saw no man or animal there along the rimrock. He got his back against a sandstone and dozed.

He didn't get this.

When he looked again, Jones was riding toward the burned farmhouse. Trundell still sat his mount in the brush. Jones poked around the ashes and walked around, and then he headed south a few miles, with Trundell still hidden and watching. The day

45

was running out, and Jones turned toward Elkhorn, riding at a lope now against the raw wind. The rise of the hills hid the lawman.

Now Trundell rode out of the brush. He circled east and then came out of the hills, coming toward Elkhorn. Parker chewed his cigar butt savagely. He was disappointed; he had thought something might come of this. He spat the cigar out and dug a hole with his toe. He pushed the cigar into that and covered it again.

He got his horse, rode west.

Cattle were moving on this side of the range. He came on a man turning some, and he saw they wore the Heart Bar Six iron. They were good stock, mostly Herefords with a few Shorthorns and very few Angus. The puncher was a young, freckle-faced man who smiled with a lopsided effect.

'Ol' Ike Savage says to turn them into the hills, an' keep them off bottom grass, an' that's what we're doin'. You're Parker, ain't you?'

Parker nodded. He turned and looked at the rimrock behind and above them. He saw a distant rider wheeling across a high ridge. Both he and the puncher looked at the man, who was only a pinpoint against the hills.

'One of your men?' asked Parker.

'None of our hands ridin' up there.'

'Recognize him?'

The puncher shook his head. 'Too far

away, Parker.'

Parker moved his slow glance across the hills behind the man, his eyes running to a point overlooking Muleshoe. Evidently the rider—whoever he was—had been over him all the time, hidden by the ledge from Parker's glasses. Parker felt an uneasiness creep across his back. The hills rose behind the rider and he fell out of sight.

'So long, cowboy,' he said.

He swung along a downhill trail, cutting north to run around the toe of the hill. A gnome rode out, bent and twisted on his horse, and lifted one hand slowly, peering up at Parker. He was the Sioux known as Crazy Springs.

'How, Parker.'

There was a silence. Parker felt the sharp scrutiny of the Sioux buck's dark, aged eyes.

'You work for old Ike Savage, huh?'

'No.'

The eyes showed something. 'Oh, I thought you do.'

Parker turned his horse flatly. 'Look, fellow. I rode out to see Savage yesterday to tell him I wanted no part in this. I run a table down in Elkhorn. I didn't want any trouble. I ride neither side.'

'Me see.'

Crazy Springs scowled.

★　　★　　★

Parker touched his horse and rode around the bend. He looked back once. The old buck still sat and looked at him.

Jetta Savage was turning cattle up out of a creek bottom. She rode a close saddle, and Parker found himself admiring her. She turned up her small, freckled face to him, her red lips parted a little.

'So mamma's boy is getting out in the country, huh? Good for little city boys who sit behind gambling tables all the time with yellow lamplight on them, so they tell me.'

Parker said shortly, 'You're descriptive, Miss Jetta.'

'Feel that sun,' said Jetta suddenly. 'Look at those hills.' She laughed briefly. 'You'd better get out, fellow, or you won't feel the sun long, maybe. I hear you're not liked so well down in Elkhorn.'

Parker shrugged.

'Oh, well,' stated Jetta. She dug down into her saddle-bag. 'Want a drink?'

Parker drank a little. She took a long swig, corked the bottle, put it back. 'You must think I'm a drunkard,' she said.

Parker shrugged again.

'Is that all you can do?' she demanded quickly. 'Just lift your shoulders and let them fall?'

Parker moved his horse close to hers. He put his arms around her and pulled her in and kissed her on the lips. She did not try to push away.

'Well, now,' she said, 'you've done that before, I believe.'

Parker felt a little angry with himself, but it was too late now to combat a sudden impulse that had been carried out. She was smiling at him, her lips parted a little. The hardness had left her face. But he thought, it'll come back, and it touched her again, twisting her lips.

'What's wrong with you?' he asked.

She was suddenly girlish, almost childlike. This left, and she had her tongue against her teeth, either in anger or weariness. 'He's dying, see. He's worked hard all his life. He's chased lousy dollars. He sent Connie and me off to school. Connie could take it; I couldn't. He didn't like that. Connie gets it all—lock, stock, and barrel. Or he tells me that his will is that way.'

'And that hurts you?'

'Why are we talking about this?' she said. 'Look, sonny boy, it's time you were getting back into town. There's a long night ahead of you, you know. Some of the boys are waiting to take you over your table. I might spend a few hard-earned nickels myself to see how you handle the cards. Do you think I would make a good gambler?'

'I don't know. But I do know you make a good riddle.'

She said, 'Good-bye,' and loped off,

49

swinging her lass-rope against the rumps of the steers. Parker watched her for a long moment; then he pushed on.

Other men were working Heart Bar Six cattle back into the hills. Kirt Stanton was with a man on Tumbling Creek, and he called to Parker.

'You see Jetta up ahead, gambler?'

Parker didn't like the way the range boss said gambler, but he let it ride. 'About a mile ahead.'

Stanton sat a pawing horse. 'I'd stay away from her, if I were you. You see, we're going to be married.'

Parker murmured, 'You got me wrong, fellow. Congratulations.'

Stanton looked at him. 'Thanks,' he said.

CHAPTER SEVEN

Parker washed in his room. A quick glance told him the room had not been entered during his absence, although it had been left unlocked. He rubbed on the thick towel and went into the lobby.

'There was an Indian here looking for you this afternoon,' said the clerk.

'Oh.'

'Crazy Springs, from the Heart Bar Six.'

'I saw him.'

Evidently Crazy Springs had been anxious to see him. Yet when he had met the Sioux, the gnome had been tight-lipped. Had he wanted to tell him something and then changed his mind?

He ate at the café. The more he saw of Millie Williams, the more he liked her. He liked the slowness of her speech, the way she looked at him. He caught her glance full on him, and she looked away.

Sheriff Jones sat in front of his office. Parker sat down beside him, and they watched the subtle alchemy of evening change the colors across the hills. Jones said, 'The farmers are meeting tomorrow night in Little Rock. In the schoolhouse. Somebody cut some fences last night, and Heart Bar Six cattle were in there, in a wheat field. Chopped it with their hoofs and chawed off some of the wheat.'

'Who cut the fence?'

'I don't know; wish I did.' Jones coughed and spat. 'There are lots of things around this town I don't know. Some people I can't understand, either.' He was looking at Parker.

Parker smiled. 'Just a gambler, Jones. A drifting gambler.' He remembered the grey horse with the rump markings, and he remembered how that horse and its rider had drifted by him in the snowstorm after he'd heard the shot that killed Luke Smith. The

51

sheriff had a grey like that. Maybe somebody didn't understand him, either. Parker put him down in the book as a tricky gent.

Martin Trundell locked his bank. He nodded at Jones and then at Parker. 'Now there's a fella I can't understand,' said Jones. 'He looks like a cowman—he always wears justin boots and a stetson. He even has hooks on his boots! Yet he's a banker. And a good one, I guess.'

Trundell went into the café.

Three riders came around a far building, entering the main street. Connie and Jetta Savage, and Kirt Stanton. Jones continued talking. 'Now look at those three. Stanton is crazy about Jetta, and Jetta's only crazy about herself. She's greedy and has a quick tongue and a temper that sweeps across her pretty body like a prairie fire runnin' acrost dried buffalo grass under a high wind.'

'They're to be married, I understand.'

Jones coughed again. 'I'll wait for the day,' he said.

'Connie's different,' said Parker.

'Difference between night and day. But you can't tell what Connie thinks, fella. She's quiet and thoughtful, but she has a mind. She's like a still pool sleeping under moonlight. She's deep, she's Ike Savage's daughter, just like Jetta is ol' Ike's blood.'

Parker got up. 'See you again,' he said.

He lay on his bed and dozed. Gradually the

dusk turned to night and with the night came a few night sounds. A nighthawk owl whammed overhead, dipping in flight to catch flies. The bloom of his wings entered Parker's dozings.

Parker lay for three hours thinking. He donned another suit, one he had hung in the closet to shed its wrinkles. The cut of the black coat fitted his bony shoulders perfectly. He put on a white shirt and a black bow tie and polished black boots. He lit the lamp and took a deck of cards out of his grip. He sat beside the small table and riffled them for five minutes; then he dealt twenty hands of cards.

He put the deck in the box and tossed it on the bed. He got his shoulder holster and fixed it around him and put the .32 in the spring holster. He washed his hands again and went downstairs.

Jones moved out of the shadows.

Parker said, 'Well, I'll get to work now.'

Jones looked at him steadily, 'Good luck,' he said.

*   *   *

Parker went into the café. He ordered a cup of hot coffee. Millie Williams was alone, checking her day's receipts, and he shoved out a dime.

'You're a lovely woman,' he said.

'Oh.'

53

She was pleased. She did not look up, but he saw her teeth touch her bottom lip, and he saw the faint flush that touched her cheeks. 'Parker, you made me miss my count!'

'You're still lovely.'

He finished his coffee, said, 'Well, for honest toil, a whole night's worth.' He was straight and dark, and she glanced up at him. He put his hand over hers and held it, and she looked up again.

'Parker, please.'

He felt a little baffled. He said, 'Good night, Millie.'

'Don't go away mad,' she said.

He stopped in the door and looked back. 'I won't.'

'There'll be a dance Saturday night at the schoolhouse.'

He considered. 'Business,' he said quietly. 'Saturday is always a big night for a gambler.'

'Dances run until daylight here. I'll go alone, and I'll meet you there about two. Would that be all right?'

'Don't ask such silly questions.'

Some of the tables had already started at the Double Diamond. Parker took his place against the wall and hung up a sign that said, 'Stud.' The proprietor tossed six decks of new cards on the table, the seals still unbroken.

Jed Hawkins took a seat at Parker's right. Parker said, 'Hello, Hawkins,' and tossed him a deck. Hawkins broke the seal with his thumb nail. Parker noticed that the man's nail was not broken or short, but long and well kept. He found himself wondering about that. Usually a farmer didn't pay much attention to his hands.

He glanced around as two other men, undoubtedly farmers, slipped into chairs. That left one vacant seat. Four other tables were running, two with draw poker and one with fantan. He slid the cards to a farmer and took out a small cigar and lit it. 'You deal, fellow.'

They bought chips. Each farmer took ten dollars' worth. Hawkins said, 'I'll take twenty,' and then to a farmer, 'That means I should be in longer than you two gents.'

Parker smiled, he liked this farmer. 'I'm not that bad,' he said.

The cards went out. Parker caught a king in the hole. That was a good start, and he smiled a little. He looked at a far table suddenly. Jetta Savage was playing the fantan spread. She was the only woman in the saloon.

More men came in. He glanced over his cards and met the flat gaze of Kirt Stanton. Parker nodded, and the range boss nodded back slightly. Jetta Savage was still at the fantan table.

One of the farmers dropped out. A man slid into his spot. Parker was a little surprised to see it was Martin Trundell. The banker ordered five dollars' worth and Parker riffled out the chips. The gambler looked hard at the bill.

'It's good,' muttered Trundell.

Parker glanced at the man. The banker was smiling. Parker said, 'Just an old habit, Trundell. A gambler's habit.'

'A banker's too,' said Trundell.

*   *   *

Trundell was a good poker player; so was Jed Hawkins. The other farmer fell out, grumbling a little. Parker saw that Jetta Savage had noticed the empty chair at his table and had started toward it. He was glad when a man slid into the seat. Jetta returned her attention to fantan.

Parker took in a pot by the strength of a strong hole card. Crazy Springs walked by, glanced at him with inscrutable dark eyes. The buck nodded and went to the bar.

'What's he doing in here?' asked Trundell. 'Never have seen that Indian in a saloon. Usually he stays close to Ike Savage.'

'What happened to his back?' asked Hawkins.

Parker listened to Trundell's explanation that the Indian had undoubtedly been born a hunchback, and he guessed Trundell was right. The buck took a drink at the bar and went outside, glancing at Parker once. Parker wondered if he wanted to see him. He couldn't leave his game now. The buck went outside.

The clock showed after midnight. Parker felt tired. He would close his table at two. At one-thirty, Hawkins dropped out, some thirty dollars to the good. Trundell had lost almost a hundred.

Jetta Savage took Hawkins' chair.

Parker said, 'Please don't.'

'You run an open game.' Jetta's voice was too husky.

Parker stood up. He beckoned to the owner of the Double Diamond. 'I don't deal to women,' he said. 'I never have; I never will. And this one is getting drunk.'

The saloon heard his words.

The heavy proprietor hurried over. He said, 'Jetta, please. Get a drink and go home. I knew your dad—'

'This is an open game,' she maintained.

The saloon was silent.

Kirt Stanton left a poker table and came close. He said, 'If she wants to play poker, she's over twenty-one. Don't run too high a game, Parker.'

Parker drove his right fist forward. Stanton went back, his lip cut. Parker followed, punching. Stanton went into the bar, held himself. He reached for his gun. But Parker had the .32 out.

Jetta watched, eyes bright.

57

Stanton wet his lips and spat out blood. Sheriff Jones came in. He said, 'Parker, holster that gun.' There was steel in the sick man. 'Jetta, get out of here. Stanton, take her out; somebody has to take care of you.'

Jetta muttered, 'You'll pay for this, tinhorn,' and her face was savage. She went out with Stanton.

Parker said, 'Thanks, Jones.'

'My job.'

Parker went back to his table. His game was broken up. Trundell was dark and stormy. Parker remembered that this banker and the range boss had been together when he had ridden into Elkhorn.

He called in his chips and racked them and gave the rack to the Double Diamond proprietor, who counted out his change, taking the ten per cent cut. The heavy man said, 'A word of advice, friend. Watch this Stanton man.'

'Gracias'.

Parker took a short beer at the bar. He wanted the turbulence to die out in him. Maybe he shouldn't have hit Stanton, but they had pushed him hard on this range. He felt the shaky feeling leave him.

Gamblers were closing shop; the Double Diamond was almost deserted. Parker saw the buck, Crazy Springs, walk past the open door. He went out and saw the buck go into an alley, evidently heading for the livery barn. He followed him.

He was walking past a dark building when they jumped him. He fought back, there in the darkness, but they had clubs. The whole thing was confused, uncertain. It happened so fast that he could not recognize the men. But he saw that one was short and squat.

Then he lost consciousness.

CHAPTER EIGHT

Parker came to with a pounding headache and blood in his mouth. He sat up by sheer effort. Giddiness swarmed in on him and his brain spun, almost dropping him again in the alley. He put his head in his hands and held it and finally the dizziness left. He got to his feet.

His first thought was that he had been slugged and robbed, but a search of his pockets revealed he still had his wallet, fat from his night's gambling. He had his watch, too—a gold-cased timepiece that was rather valuable. Evidently his assailants had not wanted his belongings.

His head ached and he held it, leaning against a building. His watch showed him he had been out about ten minutes. He pulled his hands back from his eyes and saw the carboard that lay at his feet, white in the moonlight. He bent and got it and read the printing on it:

Parker:
You are in danger on this range. Be smart and saddle your horse and ride out. We'll guarantee you a safe ride out of Muleshoe Basin. Take our offer and be wise and stay alive.

He examined the sign carefully. The thing that struck him as odd was that it was printed, not scrawled with crayon or pencil. He turned it in his fingers. It was printed on glossy stock, a good poster-paper.

Parker straightened his suit and brushed the dust off it. He went to the town windmill and washed in the horse trough, using his handkerchief as a towel. Somebody wanted him off this Muleshoe range and they were warning him. Next time there would be no warning, he figured; there would be a shot in the back.

He remembered seeing a dim, squat figure swinging one of the thin clubs. Had the wielder of that club been the Indian, Crazy Springs? Parker wished he knew for sure. He put the name of the Indian down in his mind as a dangerous character. He would watch him from now on.

The water felt good against his face. He had caked blood on his hair. He washed it off and combed his hair. He straightened his

60

flat-brimmed stetson and brushed some more dust from him. The windmill was pumping cold water out of the earth, and it flowed through a pipe into the trough. He drank, holding his mouth to the pipe. The water was cold and good. He felt better.

He didn't know just what to do. There was no use looking for his assailants. They had either left town, he figured, or they had holed up somewhere, keeping off the street. He went to the livery barn. He had intended to question the old hostler, but the man was drunk and dead to the world, lying on his office floor with his mouth open as he snored. Parker looked at him and smiled in pity and sympathy. Was the man never sober?

He looked at the horses in the barn. He found out nothing from them; he knew none of them except Sheriff Ed Jones' grey with dark rump markings. He looked at that horse for some time. He must have been mistaken; surely Sheriff Jones had not killed Luke Smith. No, that was the horse he had seen that day of the freak spring blizzard.

His thoughts kept returning to the Indian called Crazy Springs. What had the buck wanted to see him about? Parker made a mental resolution to question the Indian the next time he saw him. He was sure the buck knew something.

He went out on the main street again, going toward his hotel. Sheriff Jones came out of the shadows. Parker turned and instinctively reached for his shoulder holster before he recognized the lawman. Jones sighed.

'A friend of yours, Parker.'

Parker said, 'Have I got any friends here?'

Jones looked at him for a long time. 'What's that you carry in your hand, sir? And what happened to your face?'

They went to Jones' office. The sheriff sat and looked at the floor, and Parker watched him as he told of the beating he had taken. Parker watched the man's face, noting the high dark marks of death on his cheeks, but he saw no change come over the man.

'Why would somebody beat you?'

'Could you guess as to that, Sheriff?'

'Stanton didn't like that pile-driver right you used on him. But still I don't think that Stanton is the kind to jump a man in an alley and smash him down with a billy-club.' Jones looked at the printed placard.

'That's been printed for some time,' said Parker. 'The ink is dry and strong. That means that somebody has been planning this for some time, a day or two anyway.'

'That puts Stanton out,' said Jones.

Parker nodded. His head throbbed. 'Then who is there left?' he asked. 'Who would want to beat me—and why?'

Jones said, 'Are you a special lawman?'

Parker smiled. 'No.' He added, 'What's

wrong with this range, Jones? There's an undercurrent here, and it's fast and it's dangerous—a man can feel it. What is it?'

'I can't feel it,' said Jones.

Parker studied the stern, lined face. Jones could feel it all right; he had his foot braced in it. Yet he didn't want to talk about it. Parker decided to shut up; he had already said too much. He got to his feet, and his knees were still uncertain. He said good night and left.

Elkhorn was silent under the night's late push. A pony stood in front of a saloon, dark under the moon, his owner inside in a private poker game.

Trundell stood in front of the bank, almost hidden by shadows. Parker said, 'You're up late, friend,' and Martin Trundell moved closer, his spur rowels chiming a little, making a musical silvery sound.

'I had a hard time sleeping, got up and went for a walk. I have found that the older a man gets, the less sleep he needs.'

'I've noticed that.'

Trundell was looking at Parker's face. Parker made no offer to explain the cause of his swollen features. Trundell did not ask him.

'You like this town?' asked the banker.

'Another town. A place to run a game. I'll be here until the games run out. A man rides the current for a while in each town, and then

63

for some reason his popularity wanes, and it's time to move on.'

'The gold towns are booming. There's Zortman and Landusky in the Little Rockies. And Wood Mountain across the Line is going strong.'

'I might go there,' said Parker. 'That is, after a week or so.'

He had the impression that Trundell was driving at something; evidently the man wanted him out of town. Trundell glanced down at the placard he carried, but Parker held it so the banker could not see the printing.

'The Indian was down the street a while ago,' said Trundell. 'He asked me about you, and wanted to know where he could find you?'

'That right?'

'I told him you had a room at the hotel. I don't know where he went from when I saw him. Maybe he left town. I saw a humped-over man leave right after that on horseback, heading toward the Savage rancho.'

Parker thought, He said rancho, instead of ranch. And you only hear that down on the Mexican border and in California. But what did that tell him? Nothing except that Martin Trundell had evidently spent some time in the Southwest or on the Pacific Coast. And who hadn't?

Trundell moved off, saying, 'Good night, sir.' Parker went toward the hotel, wondering about this night and its doings. Well, the night would be over soon. Dawn was just an hour or so away. He'd sleep and then get out to the farmers' meeting on the Little Rock school-grounds. He was tired and he ached and he wanted a bed. He needed a headache powder too.

Parker saw a man coming down the street behind him. He wondered if the fellow was trailing him, and he pulled back into the shadows and let him pass, some twenty feet away. But the man kept to the open road, not to the shadows. Parker recognized him as the farmer, Jed Hawkins. He watched Hawkins go into the hotel.

Parker stood silent for five minutes, then went to the hotel. Hawkins was dozing in the lobby, sitting in a deep chair. There was a small kerosene lamp that sent dancing shadows and light across the lobby. There was nobody behind the desk and a sign was hung over the register that said SOLD OUT FOR THE NIGHT.

Parker said, 'Sleepy, Hawkins?'

Hawkins came awake. 'You walk light,' he said. 'I was only dozing and I didn't hear you. I didn't want to ride all the distance to my farm, so thought I'd bed down in a room for the rest of the night. But I see they're all taken.'

65

'There's an extra cot in my room.'

Hawkins yawned. 'Thanks, Parker, thanks. But there's a lot of hay in the livery barn; I can bed down there, fellow. But thanks again.'

'You're welcome,' said Parker.

'I'll call you on that,' said Hawkins. He got to his feet. 'Say, Parker, I saw that Indian of Ike Savage's—that Crazy Springs fellow—and he wanted to see you, he said. Oh, that was fifteen, twenty minutes ago. I told him you had a room here, and he headed this way.'

Parker scowled. 'What does he want? I'm going to talk to him.'

They went up the creaking stairs. Parker stopped inside the door, Hawkins beside him.

Crazy Springs lay on his belly, one arm bent under him. There was blood under his head and under his buckskin jacket. His moccasins and buckskin shotgun pants had a little blood on them, too. There had been a struggle in the room. The bed was messed, the one chair over-turned.

Parker knelt beside the man. He had been knifed. Parker got to his feet and looked at Jed Hawkins. 'He don't want to see me now,' he said.

CHAPTER NINE

Hawkins said, 'Knifed, huh? But why and by who?' He looked at Parker.

'I don't know. Do you?'

'How would I know?'

Parker murmured, 'Just a question, fellow, just a question.' He walked around the room. He didn't know who had killed the Indian, but he knew Crazy Springs had been murdered to keep him from talking.

The room told Parker nothing. There had been a struggle; evidently it had been short and violent. But beyond that Parker knew nothing. He knelt beside the man while Hawkins went after Sheriff Ed Jones. Crazy Springs had been knifed four times.

Jones looked the room over carefully, but if he found anything, Parker did not know what it was.

'Take him down to my office,' the sheriff said.

Dawn was lighting the hills when they carried the dead Sioux into Jones' office, where they laid him on the floor. Jones asked questions of Hawkins and Parker, and Parker told him exactly what he had done after leaving the lawman. Hawkins said he had been dozing in the lobby, which Parker substantiated.

Parker went back to his room. The clerk was mopping the blood off the floor. He offered to place the gambler in another room but Parker didn't care to move. The man got the floor clean and left with his scrub buckets.

Parker undressed and went to bed. He jacked a chair under the doorknob and pulled the blind low to shut out the rising sun. He went to sleep easily. At three he was awake, washing and dressing. He went down to the café and ate. Millie was home, the waitress said; Parker missed her.

Parker loafed around town. Everybody knew of Crazy Springs' death and they looked at him queerly. He went to the Double Diamond and told the proprietor that he might not deal in that evening. The man said that was all right. Play would be dull this night because the farmers were going to the meeting at Little Rock. Dusk finally came. Parker ate late. When it was dark, he went to the barn and saddled his horse and rode south. Once in the hills, he cut back. He rode into the buck-brush behind the Heart Bar Six ranch-house at about nine o'clock.

He tied his horse there and went ahead on foot. He settled in the brush, ears keen, and watched the bunkhouse with its lights, the cabins of Jetta and Connie. Only Connie's had a light.

He went forward, leaving the brush, and

pushed against the back door. It was open, and he went inside into the dark kitchen, went down a darkened hall.

Savage's door was closed. Parker opened the door.

Savage lay flat on his back, one hand on the white quilt. Grizzled iron-grey whiskers sprouted out of his flat cheeks and thin chin. The lamplight showed the hardness of his sunken eyes. Parker saw that the other claw was under the quilt and he saw the outline of a gun, possibly a .45. He saw that bulky bump move down, and the claw came up and rested beside the other sunken hand.

Savage sent sharp eyes at Parker's face. 'You've been ganged up on?'

'How did you know I was ganged on?'

'I take you for a hard man. No man could trim you that way unless he had an ally in another man and another ally in the dark. Why do you come to me? What have you found out?'

Parker confessed, 'I have found out nothing. I know nothing more than when I saw you last. Perhaps I will find nothing. Perhaps I should ask you to release me from our agreement.'

'You want to ride on?'

Parker fingered his tender skull. 'Do you think I would run after they treated me this way? Do you think I am a coward?'

'But you have considered running out.'

'Yes, I had thought of that. But when they ganged me—Crazy Springs is dead, but you know that.'

Surprise ran across the lacklustre eyes. 'Nobody told me. I wondered where he was. Where was he killed, and how, and when?'

Parker told him.

'He was my friend,' said Ike Savage slowly. 'I have known him for years—fifty years, I guess. Now he is dead because of me.'

'Why do you say that?'

'He knew something he wanted to tell to you. That is why they killed him.'

'Who are they?' asked Parker.

Ike Savage's voice held a harsh note. 'I don't know. How would I know? I'm flat on my back; I can't get around. If I could ride a horse—if I could walk—'

Parker waited, nerves cold. This place was eerie. 'Stanton is moving your cattle out, sir,' he said. He told him about seeing Heart Bar Six cattle being shoved back into the hills. He told about hitting Stanton and how Jetta had tried to crowd into his table.

'You hit the wrong person, Parker. You should've hit her!'

Parker shook his head.

'What's behind this?' asked Parker.

White teeth came out and settled on a whiskery underlip. 'I don't know, Parker. There's something—something big. Is it cattle? No, I don't think so. But what is it?

Evidently Crazy Springs knew what it was. That knowledge died with him when the knife ripped into him. But who handled that knife?'

Parker moved back against the door.

Savage said, 'You'll stay, then?'

Parker looked at the broken, thin man. He saw the slender form under the covers, saw the covers hug the contour. 'I'll stay,' he said.

He rode to the Little Rock school.

★　　★　　★

He got there late. He was thinking of Millie Williams as he left saddle. The lamps in the school threw shadows and light across the buckbrush which surrounded the creek that skipped its cold way down to Milk River. A man could tie on to Millie, and he'd have a rock to hold him to a stern way. She was solid and good and bright, and a man could ask no more.

And then he smiled.

Rigs were tied in the willows and at the hitchrack in front of the log building. A pole fence made of peeled diamond willows encircled the single-room rural school. Parker went across the worn porch and stepped inside the open door.

Somebody whispered, 'Hello, Parker.'

Jed Hawkins sat on a bench toward the front. He moved to one side, and Parker sat down beside him. A man was talking about his fence being cut. He was flushed, his face the color of a cooked red beet, and he pounded the lectern that stood on the raised platform.

Hawkins whispered, 'Jesse Hoggins, from Line Crick. He's got a hen on, it looks like.'

Parker listened to the farmer demand that the farmers, as a group, settle with old Ike Savage and his Heart Bar Six men. He got the swift impression that this meeting should never have been held, that it was useless.

Hoggins stopped, his flow of words through, and asked for comment. There was a moment of silence, and then Jed Hawkins stepped up and asked the chairman for the floor. He got it. Parker watched the farmer walk to the front of the hall. Hawkins wet his lips slowly, running his tongue around his mouth, and then he spoke in a firm, convincing voice. Parker noticed he used good English, and his talk was forceful and to the point.

Hawkins asked them to be tolerant, to give the Heart Bar Six time to move its cattle back into the hills. He told them that a range war meant death, ugly death, and he appealed to the women to haul their men into line.

'You've said that before,' hollered a man, breaking in.

Hawkins waited, his face calm. Another man said to Parker, 'He's talked peace for months, and it's gettin' tiresome.'

'Peace isn't tiresome,' murmured Parker.

'He always advocates wait, wait, wait. We're getting tired of waiting. What do you say, Parker? You've been around.'

'It's your problem, fellow.'

The meeting broke up, nothing accomplished. Parker and Jed Hawkins rode toward town and came to the farmer's homestead. Hawkins said good night, and Parker rode on alone. Dawn was not far distant. Parker was tired. He stabled his horse and fed him and went to bed. But first, he jacked the chair under the door knob.

CHAPTER TEN

When Parker had come to the Heart Bar Six, Connie Savage had been coming toward the house. She saw the movement of the dark man, and she drew back into a concealing shadow. She did not recognize him right away as Parker. The night was thick and the distance a trifle too far.

She saw the man go into the house by the back door. She moved ahead and waited, hidden in the brush, and she saw Parker come out. Then she heard a horse moving somewhere, and the sound grew less and less and then died. She went around the house and came in from the front. She went to her father's room.

'What do you want?' he asked.

'I just came to see if you were all right.'

Savage's dull eyes were bright with a sudden tenderness. He remembered when this girl had been a child and he remembered her sweetness.

'Where is your sister?'

'In her cabin.'

Savage turned his gaunt head and glanced out the window. 'Her cabin is dark,' he said. 'Does she ride tonight?'

Connie looked at him steadily. She jerked herself back to reality. 'I was day-dreaming,' she said. She asked, 'Where would she go?'

Savage never answered that.

'Where would she ride?' she repeated.

Connie walked to the window.

'My sister reminds me of a bitter young animal,' she said. 'She paces her cage and her steps are tireless.'

'I have no pen around her.'

Connie rubbed her firm chin. 'No, you haven't, Father, but she has. She drives herself. She doesn't let herself rest. What is she after? I don't know. She doesn't know. She just paces, and the cage is imaginary.'

Savage watched her.

'We're all that way, I guess,' she said.

'Not all of us, Connie.' His eyes were points of steel that followed her as though she were a magnet turning them.

'You were that way. You were fierce and savage, and you fought to hold this land, to build up this ranch. You fought hard and you fought clean.'

'Yes, I fought clean.'

She stopped, rubbed her chin. She had said the wrong word. She decided to leave and wondered why she had come.

'Good night, Dad.'

'Wait a minute,' he said.

She stopped, put one hand against the door jamb. She was pretty and she was his daughter; he felt a quick stab of pride.

'Why did you come, Connie?'

'To see you, of course.'

His eyes followed her again. He said, 'I see,' and then, 'Close the door, girl, and sleep well tonight.'

'How could one sleep in such a house!' she stormed.

She went down the hall. When she stepped into the night, the lines had come back deep and swift, and she closed her mouth and brought this hardness to the surface. For a while, in there, she had felt a bit of pity.

She looked at Jetta's cabin. She was in there, Connie was sure—was sitting there, rocking as an old woman rocks, and she would be knitting. Jetta could knit in the dark. Jetta had the eyes of a cat. She would sit there and knit and she would rock the way

75

an old lady rocks. ⸚

She stood by the barn door.

Finally the bunkhouse door opened. She heard the sounds of men, their talk and loudness, and the closing door shut this off. A man came toward her. He swaggered with a short man's arrogance.

Connie said, 'Kirt Stanton.'

Stanton stopped. 'My Lord, Connie. Why do you stand there?'

'The night,' she said. 'I like the darkness.'

Stanton had settled on his thighs. 'I don't.' He spoke flatly. 'It reminds me of that day when they'll put me into a dark hole in the ground. It reminds me of how that soil will press around me and take me into its darkness.'

'You won't regret it.'

Stanton hunkered, silent. He rolled a cigarette and stuck it in his mouth and the match showed the lines of his face, its lack of character. His right eye was a little black. Connie thought again of Parker. Parker's fist had run that ring around the range boss' right eye.

There was no character to this man. He had gone up by sheer work, not by intelligence. He was faithful; he made her think of a dog, a homely dog that you had given a home to, that you had fed well and let lie beside your fire. But he was dangerous because of this faithfulness.

Jetta was shoving him along. She wanted no part of him; yet she played with him, presumably to feed some blind ego. Stanton did not know this, but Connie knew it, and the other Heart Bar Six men knew it. Stanton had his cigarette going. He got up and said, 'Well, I'll take a look at the horses and then turn in. I wouldn't stand too long in this wind, Connie.'

Connie said, 'Good night, Kirt,' and went to her cabin.

She blew out the lamp. The darkness was close. This was wearing on her, running across her like wind-blown grains of sand, one after another, moving across her and wearing her down. She went to Jetta's cabin. She was lifting her knuckles to knock when Jetta said, 'Come in, Connie.'

Connie went inside. She shut the door, leaned against the casing and looked at the shadowy form of her sister. Jetta was rocking, rocking and knitting. Connie could hear the slight rub of the steel needles through the wool. The room was a little close and the air was not too good.

'How did you know I was outside, Jetta?'

'I have ears,' said Jetta. 'Sometimes I wonder about my hearing; I can hear almost anything.'

'Crazy Springs must have heard something, too. Something he shouldn't have heard; or maybe he saw it.'

Jetta had no answer.

Connie thought that perhaps she would tell her about the coming of Parker to the Heart Bar Six, then decided against it. This girl knew too much already, she figured; why tell her more? Parker was in enough danger as it was without her adding more to his shoulders. She would keep his visit secret.

Jetta asked, 'How's Ike?'

Connie was slow to answer. 'He's just the same, I'd say. Day by day he slips and slips. He goes deeper.'

The needles clashed a little. 'Then Connie Savage will be the boss of the Heart Bar Six. She'll own the ranch all by herself.'

'I'll sign over half to you, Jetta. You know that. You've crossed the old man too many times. That's why he made out his will that way. He might change it; I've asked him to.'

'I don't give a hoot. I don't want half the place; when I take it, I take it all. Everything.'

Connie let hardness rim her voice. 'Back on the same old path,' she said. 'Who killed Crazy Springs?'

The needles were purring. Steel rubbing against wool and steel. 'I don't know, Connie.'

'You lie, Jetta!'

'All right, then; you're right. I lie. Does that satisfy you?'

Connie was facing a stone wall. She had

78

faced it before. She had tried to climb it before, too, but it had been too high. She did not try now. She turned and walked outside.

'Good-bye,' said Jetta.

Connie shut the door.

★ ★ ★

She stood for a moment silent and undecided. Suddenly she loathed this ranch, hated it. She went to the barn. A lantern was lighted and hung on a hook on an upright, and she walked through its yellow rays. She saddled a big black gelding and found her stirrup and rode out the back door. She headed across country at a long free lope.

She tried to lose the taste, the feel, of that room back there. Jetta's room. She tried to lose the memory of that chair rocking, of those needles punching the wool. They symbolized a number of things to her, distasteful things. First there was greed, blind, angry greed; there was hate there, too. She herself was no angel; but she wasn't always tight across her nerves, she had moments of softness.

The night air was cool. The black fell to a trot, then a running walk. He was going toward Elkhorn. She let him go that way.

When she reached Elkhorn, the town was dark. Morning was not many minutes away. She rode into the livery and tied her black horse to a manger. The old hostler was sleeping on his bunk. She leaned low and smelled his breath. There was no whisky on it. She shrugged and said, 'A miracle.'

He slept as if dead. That made her think of her father and his sunken, lifeless eyes.

She went down the silent street and went into the hotel and sat in a big chair in the lobby. She was sleepy and she caught herself dozing off. Parker found her there, sleeping in the big chair. He hesitated about waking her, but finally he shook her shoulder gently.

'Connie.'

She stretched like a sleepy, lazy cat. Her eyes were the eyes of a cat. 'I was tired, I guess. I sat down and went to sleep.'

'Have breakfast with me?'

CHAPTER ELEVEN

Martin Trundell locked the bank and went to his bachelor quarters. He debated whether to go to the café to eat or to mix up some grub at home. He decided on the latter; he ate slowly, enjoying the food and the solitude.

He finished eating and washed his dishes. Then he lit a lamp and pulled the blinds down as he took a ten-dollar bill from his wallet and held it close to the lamplight.

He let the rays run through the bill,

studied it for a full minute.

He finished his scrutiny, took another ten-dollar bill and looked at it. He laid them both on the table and studied them together. His face drew back, bringing out the high planes of his cheeks, and he sat like this for a long moment. Then he put the bills back into the wallet and restored it to his hip pocket.

He shoved back his chair and looked down at his boots in thought. He let an hour rush by and still sat there with no impatience inside of him. He lifted his eyes and looked at the clock, got to his feet and crossed the room, took a rifle from the rack on the wall.

It was a Winchester .30-30. He broke the lever and jacked the bullet out, catching it in midair. He put another cartridge into the barrel and fixed the safety catch. He shook the bullet he had jacked out, looked at it and seemed satisfied with it, so he shoved it into the magazine.

He went outside. The night was dark before the moon would rise. He had two horses in his barn; a blue roan, heavy-legged and sure, and a long-legged bay who took his head out of the manger and nuzzled him. He put his Miles City saddle on the bay, bridled the horse, put the Winchester in the saddleboot and rode out.

He did not ride up Elkhorn's main street but swung straight south, leaving the town behind, and rode across the prairie. He came to a fenced lane and rode by it. He met two rigs going to the Little Rock School. The darkness hid his identity from the farmers. He did not speak to them but rode on silently; they probably thought he was a Heart Bar Six puncher going to the home ranch. The cowpunchers seldom, if ever, wasted breath talking to a farmer, a nester.

And that was just as well.

He reached the foothills. He was on Savage range. He had seen old Ike Savage once, and his mind swept back to that day. The room had been cold and without fire. Savage had been piled over with blankets. He had asked Trundell to help him make out his will.

Trundell had done this, and he had recorded the will. The terms of it were clear in his mind even now.

A rider came ahead. Trundell drew his horse back and watched the shadowy horseman drift. He was a squat, heavy man, and Trundell recognized him as a farmer named André. Trundell had met the man once or twice and wondered about him. He had no desire to meet him now.

He watched André head toward the Little Rock school. Then the night took the farmer and kept him. Trundell seemed undecided about his next move. He decided to go to the schoolhouse. He did not ride down and tie his horse with those of the farmers, but kept on the ridge south of the building that nestled in

82

the cotton-woods and box elder trees. He kept as high as possible on the ridge, wanting nobody behind him. He left his horse in the sandstones; there the beast would be shielded from the high, raw wind. He took his rifle and went ahead and settled down and looked at the light in the schoolhouse below.

Rigs were coming in. Below him people were talking and he caught the sounds of their words, distant and indistinct. The lamplight showed a squat man when the door opened. Despite the distance, Trundell thought that man was André. André went inside as did other men and women.

The wind was cold. Trundell thought of his warm bed in Elkhorn. A man will put himself up to a lot of discomfort and cold just for a few filthy dollars. He could have been home in bed and been warm, but here he was, out on the silent hills with a raw wind against him.

An hour or so went by.

Finally he saw another rider come into the clearing in front of the schoolhouse. The man left his horse, and when he opened the door the lamplight showed him to be the gambler, Parker. Parker went inside. Trundell was frowning now. What was Parker doing with these farmers? And hadn't he ridden from the direction of the Heart Bar Six? The banker wrestled mentally with these thoughts.

A side door opened and a man came out

alone. He got his horse and rode up the slope, following a short trail into the mountains. He passed about a hundred feet north of the banker, who sat there and watched him in the moonlight. The man was André, and Trundell caught his breath. Maybe the night would not be wasted, at that; he hoped not.

André rode at a fast lope. This was a short cut that led across the neck, then went down into the basin again. It ran past the Heart Bar Six ranchhouse. Trundell followed him with the moonlight as an ally. The banker kept to the ridges and he had to hit the trail fast, for the hunchback below rode with high stirrups. But Trundell kept the stride. The hours ran out and numbered about three. Trundell saw another rider on that downtrail, a rider going toward Elkhorn. Was that Connie Savage? He let a thin smile touch him. This night was holding some interest, at that.

Connie Savage ran into the night and became lost. She was out of this picture temporarily. She was going to Elkhorn. Why? Trundell put his attention on André. He followed the hunchback.

*　　*　　*

André was going toward Crystal Springs, and Trundell remembered that a farmer had told him there were Heart Bar Six cattle bunched there. The banker was on the rimrock when the man rode down on the small herd of about two hundred head. André rode around the cattle and talked to a rider there against the far cutbank. Trundell waited.

Now another rider swept across the night, coming from the Heart Bar Six ranch. This rider moved in with the other two and then the trio swung out, going down toward the basin proper. They rode fast, and the moonlight showed the thin lift of dust behind their horses.

Trundell moved, too. He had his rifle out of scabbard and the weapon was lying across the fork of his saddle, his hands on it. He gained a high point where the wind beat against igneous rock and he waited there, hidden from the eyes below.

One of the riders was André, Trundell was sure of that. Now what was this humpback farmer doing with two Heart Bar Six riders? That didn't make sense; a farmer with the cowmen. Somebody was getting a big double-cross here, the banker figured.

But who were the other two riders? Trundell could not make them out there in the shifting shadows of the night. Now the trio below rode slower. They came to a fence, and Trundell knew it was the fence of Jesse Hoggins, the Line Creek farmer. Hoggins had his corn knee high. The trio spread out and each came to the fence.

The horses came to the fence, stopped, and

stood silent. Then their riders pushed them down the fence a way, and they stood silent again. The three horses turned then and the trio rode back to the Heart Bar Six cattle. Trundell thought he caught the reflection of moonlight on steel. Was it the steel of a gun barrel or was it the shiny steel of new fence-cutter pliers?

It could be either, he decided. He wished he could learn the identity of the two Heart Bar Six riders. He left his horse and went down on foot, carrying his rifle. He slid in loose shale and tripped on a root, falling into some mulberry bushes. The sharp thongs stung him and he cursed under his breath. Ten minutes later he was settled in the brush, watching the draw.

Somewhere cattle were moving.

He waited, his face set. Cattle came trotting around the bend, their slobber plain in the moonlight. Trundell's face was cast in bronze. He recognized André, recognized another rider as Kirt Stanton. But the third was too far away and across the herd. He could not make out that rider's identity.

They were putting the cattle through the cut wires. The cattle moved out, fanned into the field, and started to graze. They would cut this corn crop down to nothing in a few hours. By sunup the corn crop would be done, and it was too late to replant. Jesse Hoggins would really have something to kick about now. Trundell wondered if the farmer would go on the warpath.

I'd still like to identify that other rider, he thought.

He could hear cattle tearing into the tender corn stalks. The riders bunched and sat in the brush for a while, looking at the cattle moving across the plowed area. Then they turned and rode off. They parted, and two rode toward the Heart Bar Six, and André rode south. Trundell went to his horse and followed the farmer. Again he kept to the high reaches of the hills.

André was heading for his homestead. A few miles further on, Trundell drew in and watched the man ride into the yard of the homestead. Here stood a log house and log barn and a pig-pen. Night was changing slowly to day. Trundell saw him water the cow and milk her; then he fed the calf and pigs. André went into the house; Trundell waited for two hours. Smoke came lazily out of the chimney as the man cooked breakfast. Then that smoke died; André did not come out.

Trundell left his horse there. He went down and came in beside the cabin, glanced into the corner of a dirty window. The cabin consisted of one room containing a stove, a table, some rough furniture and plenty of dirt. There was a cot against the far corner but nobody was on it. The cabin was empty of human occupation. And that brought a frown to Trundell's wide forehead; he had seen André enter the cabin—and the man had not come out—still he wasn't in the cabin.

Trundell felt a sudden fear. Had the homesteader gone out without his noticing him—was he behind him now? Trundell went to his horse. He met no opposition as he found his stirrup. He rode toward Elkhorn.

He hit a long lope. By the time he reached town, it would be almost time to open his bank. He was puzzled; he couldn't understand that cabin. He must have been wrong. André must have been in that bed.

He remembered that the bed had been heaped with dirty blankets and quilts. The man must have been under those and asleep. The light had been very dim in the cabin. That was it, he thought: André was asleep under those covers.

He single-footed his horse down the main street. People were moving on the street, and he nodded to them. He was tired. He went home and shaved and went to the bank. A townsman came in, and his day had started.

'You look sleepy, Trundell,' the man joked.

The banker smiled a little. 'I'm always sleepy,' he said.

CHAPTER TWELVE

Parker and Connie Savage had breakfast together at the Elkhorn Café where Millie Williams waited on them. Parker thought he saw a shade of annoyance creep across Millie's eyes when she saw them enter together, but he was not sure. Connie was a big cat who settled opposite in the booth and looked at him through lynx-like eyes.

'I'm still tired,' she said.

Parker said, 'Chairs aren't nice to sleep on. Haven't you got a bed at the ranch?' He made the question light.

She had pulled up a veil around her and his question did not pierce it. Daylight had changed her thoughts and she was tough again. 'I'd hate to marry a man like you,' she said.

'You won't,' Parker assured her. 'You're too smart; you'd want a man you could push. There's no push in me.'

'Egotistic?'

Parker let his shoulders fall. 'No, not necessarily.'

She was looking out the window. A farmer was coming into town at a wild lope, his old horse lathered and with tired knees. He left the horse in front of Sheriff Ed Jones' office and stood in front of Jones, who sat on the bench as usual. 'That's the farmer they call Hoggins, isn't it? Jesse Hoggins?'

'I think that's his name.'

Millie was delivering their coffee. She stood and watched Hoggins gesture to Sheriff Jones. 'He seems worried,' she said. 'Wonder if anything is wrong?'

'Hard to tell in this town,' said Parker.

Millie went back into the kitchen. Hoggins and Sheriff Jones walked down the street, the farmer leading his horse, the sheriff still listening. They went into the livery barn.

The sheriff came out with a black horse and went into saddle. Hoggins found his stirrup and they loped out together. Martin Trundell had left his bank, and now Parker saw the banker stand in the doorway and watch the two ride out. Parker also saw that the Heart Bar Six range boss, Kirt Stanton, stood in front of the livery barn. Connie saw him, too.

'What's he doing in town?'

'In town most of the time,' said Parker.

Stanton settled down with his back to the livery barn wall.

Parker left Connie at the café. He went to his room, got the placard that he had found on himself when the thugs had beaten him, and cut out some of its letters. He took these to the local printer and asked him if he had printed them. The man took the material between his ink-stained fingers and looked at it for some time.

'Where did you get this?' he asked.

'Don't ask questions. Just tell me if you printed those letters.'

The man shook his head. 'No, I didn't print them.' He said they were in some type face that he didn't have in his case. He named the type face, but that made little sense to Parker. One thing did strike him odd, though. The printer didn't know where the letters had been printed and he didn't know what kind of a press had put them out. He was sure that they had been printed outside the state—possibly in a big city like Chicago—for this was a special press job with a special type.

'That looks like it came from a very good press,' he said. 'Look at the back of that paper—see how clean and smooth the back is? That means that the press has touched the paper very lightly, and there are not many presses that can be regulated down so light in the feed-touch.'

Parker thanked him and went outside, slightly befuddled. This didn't make sense to him. Here he had found that placard on him and it had his name printed on it. Yet the man said that evidently it was done on a special press out of the state. The printer must have been wrong.

He stopped in front of Trundell. 'Where did the sheriff go with that farmer?' he asked.

'I don't know.'

Parker looked at the south hills. He noticed that, in addition to a Colt .45 on his right hip, this banker carried a hide-out gun under his coat. Why all the artillery? Did he expect a bank hold-up or was he just ready if one occurred?

'I might get some printing done,' said Parker. 'Some cards. Gamblers seem to carry them nowadays. Is this shop here pretty good?'

'Should be. That printer used to work for the Bureau of Engraving in Washington, D.C., I understand. He should know his stuff.'

'He the only printer in town?'

'The only one.'

'That ought to be recommendation enough,' said Parker. 'Just for curiosity, what is he doing running a paper in such a small town? He sure can't make any money off the local advertising, can he?'

'His health. Printer's ink is hard on a man. He's gained ten pounds in the last two months, he tells me.'

Parker went to his room. He had gained little information. The placard had been printed locally, he knew; his name had been on it. Was there another press in town nobody—no, that wasn't possible. This was a riddle.

Connie Savage stood in front of the

Mercantile. Her eyes were sharp on his and he caught the flat odor of whisky on her breath.

'You'll excuse me,' he said, 'but why do you drink, Miss Savage? Or am I intruding upon your privacy?'

'You're intruding,' she said.

He felt himself flush a little. He had put out the wrong boot first, and she had stepped on it. He should've had sense enough to keep his mouth shut. But he had expected a civil answer; they had just had breakfast together.

'I'm sorry, miss.'

She said, 'Don't go.'

Parker stopped.

She spoke quietly. 'You were out to see Ike Savage last night. I happened to see you. What did you come to see him about?'

'I'm sure you are mistaken, Miss Connie. I never rode last night. I was in my hotel room until late; then I rode out to the farmers' meeting on Little Rock. Purely out of curiosity.'

She was silent. 'I'm sorry I made a mistake,' she said.

'One up for both of us.'

Parker got his horse and rode to the south hills. The sun was warm and the earth was releasing energy. Grass was green and wheat was rushing out of the sod and ready to make heads.

He rode the ridges.

*　　*　　*

Sheriff Ed Jones and Hoggins were along the farmer's fence. Parker saw that it had been cut and cattle had moved into the cornfield. They had chopped it with their sharp hoofs and the corn had been eaten to the ground. The field was a total waste.

Sheriff Jones asked, 'Where you riding for, Parker?' He was gruff and mean and sick.

'Nowhere,' said Parker. 'Riding is a hobby with me, my recreation. Don't you like it?'

Jones said, 'I don't understand you.'

Parker smiled. 'Sometimes I don't understand myself,' he admitted.

Hoggins spoke with a naked hardness. Gone was the bluster he had shown last night at the Little Rock meeting. 'I found Heart Bar Six cattle in here this morning. Heart Bar Six men cut those wires. But what can I do? I'm one man, and Ike Savage has a bunkhouse full of gunmen. They're ready to ride against us farmers when Savage lifts a finger.'

Parker was silent.

Jones spoke. 'Swear out a warrant for the arrest of Ike Savage, Hoggins. I'll serve it.'

'You can't get him into court,' said Parker. 'He's too close to dead.'

Jones regarded him. 'What do you know about Ike Savage?'

94

Parker shrugged. 'Just what I've heard.' He turned his horse, looked at Jones. 'Don't ride me with long spurs, fellow. I'm not under your jurisdiction. I'm free to ride where I want to. Next time you see me call me "sir."'

Jones watched him ride away.

Parker went into the south hills. He was riding a hunch, and he didn't want it to get cold on him. Noon came and skipped into afternoon. Below him Heart Bar Six men worked cattle, moving the bovines deeper into the hills. This didn't make sense. Here the Heart Bar Six moved cattle, and there were Heart Bar Six cattle on Hoggins' cornfield.

Parker went down into the valley. He met Kirt Stanton and he drew his horse off the trail, his hands on the fork of his saddle. Stanton said, 'We're working cattle, man, and we don't want you in our way'

'This is government land,' said Parker meaningly.

Stanton pulled in and rolled a cigarette. Parker caught the quick impression that this man was worried; something bothered him. And with his limited mentality he could not cope with his problems. Or was this just a passing fancy? Parker asked himself. Was he wrong?

'Your cattle were on Hoggins' land,' said Parker. 'The man's fences were cut. Jones says it happened last night.'

Stanton looked down at the basin. His face was without thoughts. 'If there were Savage cattle on Hoggins' land, then the farmers have put them there. We held our herd last night with guard. Those Savage cattle had ranged up in the hills and we hadn't got to them yet. They hadn't run into the corn of their own accord.'

'What are you driving at?'

'You're a stranger here,' said Stanton. 'What does this mean to you?'

'Nothing.'

'Their game isn't hard to see,' said Stanton suddenly. 'I figure we lost a few hundred head last night. They want trouble because under its cover they can steal our cattle. Those farmers ain't honest, fellow. They're trying to drive us cowmen into an open gunfight; and when the battle goes on they'll steal our cattle because we'll be ridin' gun, not stock.'

Parker had to admit that the range boss was correct. It had been done before; he had seen it done twice himself. And if Stanton were correct, then there would be need to be a subversive element among the farmers. And that could be possible.

'What would they do with these cattle?' he asked. Stanton poked a finger to the north. 'Wood Mountain, in Canada. Ain't hard to get across that line, even with our Border

Patrol and the Mounties. That's a booming camp; will take lots of beef.'

Parker nodded.

'A day's drive,' murmured Stanton.

'Where else?'

Stanton rammed a finger southwest. 'The Little Rockies. Zortman and Landusky. Gold mad and hungry for beef. Two days' drive.'

Parker was silent.

'I'm working cattle,' said Stanton suddenly. He rode off at a lope. Parker turned his horse and rode toward Elkhorn.

CHAPTER THIRTEEN

Parker had a new hand in his poker game that night. He was a short, squat farmer, and his name was André. He had stubby fingers grimed with dirt, but they knew how to riffle cards across the green-topped table.

Parker asked, 'New here?'

André looked blank. 'I've been around for some time. Have a farm out here in the hills. It's a tough row, but what is there for a man to do?'

'Gamble.'

'With hands like that?' He held up his fingers.

Parker looked at another player. 'Two cards, huh?' He slipped them out fast, looked at André. 'Just a thought.'

The game went on. André played well; so did another farmer. One was a plunger. Parker knew where he was going to end up: broke. Probably an unmarried man with no responsibilities, he figured. Not that it made a bit of difference to him; his money was as good as anybody else's.

The plunger threw in his last five, and André took the pot. The young fellow said, 'Too much luck against me,' and left. He was a little angry. Parker didn't like people who let circumstances anger them. A man can't argue with his fate.

'Didn't like it,' murmured André.

Parker merely grunted. He had an inside flush and he pulled to it, straightening it. The game was draw with jacks or better for openers. André had opened, and Parker figured he had something. He raised; André stayed and another man raised. Parker came back; André stayed and the farmer took the pot. André raked the chips with his dirty hands.

Parker looked at his own immaculate fingernails. 'Thought you had two aces, friend, but I didn't expect you to have three. Had one myself.'

The other player bought some more chips. Parker counted them out and called the proprietor who broke the bill. The game went on again. Parker had one eye on the front door. Farmers were coming in and Saturday night should be big in this burg. Still he kept thinking of Wood Mountain and the gold dust there. But he was doing all right here—from the monetary point of view.

André murmured, 'Your play.'

Parker dropped out. He saw Jed Hawkins and he lifted his head, nodding to the man. Hawkins came over and took a seat and bought in. He handed Parker twenty dollars, two ten-dollar bills. He nodded at André, who returned the greeting with a short, 'Well, another sucker, Parker.'

Parker had settled down to straight poker. He was watching every man at the table: slight mannerisms betrayed them—André had a habit of biting his lip when he got a poor hand. Probably nobody but Parker would have noticed this, but he had faced thousands across the green-top in Las Vegas, in Rio, in Tucson, just to mention a few of the scattered gambling dens that had seen his presence.

At midnight the run had quieted down and most of the farmers had left. They made it a dealer's choice game, running between draw and stud poker. Only André and Hawkins stayed with Parker. Play ran out on other tables. The faro dealer locked his box. Some of the onlookers crowded around Parker's table.

André said, 'Don't stand behind me,' and a

farmer moved, grumbling.

Trundell came in, stood and watched. Parker looked up. 'There's a vacant seat, sir,' he said.

'Too fast company for me,' said Trundell. 'I get in there and my stockholders wouldn't have any receipts left in the bank.'

Parker thought, I believe that's the first time I've ever seen him smile, and he put out four chips. André called and raised and Jed Hawkins slowly admitted that he would drop out. Parker checked André, and André had the cards. The stocky farmer was some ahead, about two hundred dollars. Hawkins was in for a hundred or so, but he could stand it—he had won to date. The money had come out of the pockets of the other two farmers, for Parker was over a hundred ahead, too.

'That cleans me,' said Hawkins.

Parker asked, 'More chips?'

Hawkins leaned back in his chair. 'All right, ten worth.' He took the bill from his vest pocket and tossed it out and Parker counted his chips. Parker flattened the bill without looking at it and put in in his leather apron. The game went on. Hawkins was running muddy luck, and he went out again. Parker glanced at the clock. 'Two,' he said. 'That time, André.'

'I'm ahead,' said André. 'I'll quit.' He got to his feet and smiled, the effort breaking his wrinkled skin. He stretched. 'Reckon I'll ride out home, late as it is. Comin' with me, Hawkins?'

'I'll stay in,' said Hawkins.

André went outside, Hawkins following. Parker counted his money out on the bar, took his cut, and walked into the cool night. Trundell stood and talked to Ed Jones, who sat beside his office. Parker wondered if the lawman ever slept. Trundell moved off, going toward his home, and Jones looked at Parker, who stood beside him.

'Any luck?'

'A little.'

Jones held his bandanna over his mouth and coughed. 'They're bitin' deeper each day. They're like buzzards.'

Parker realized there were two men dying on this range. One was an old cowman, a man who had driven Texas longhorns up the Powder Trail into this section; this cowman lay thin and wasted and near the border-line, and he cursed the flesh he had brought on this earth. The other was this lawman, sick and without hope because he would not allow himself to hope. Parker had a queer thought. Jones would die because he wanted to die; he would die because he judged he had seen enough of life, he had breathed enough good air.

Jones asked suddenly, 'Why do you stay here, Parker?'

'To gamble, of course.'

Jones coughed again. 'Wood Mountain has wild games with fortunes on the green. A good gambler goes where the money is. This is peanut money here.'

'Enough here for me.'

Jones looked at him.

Parker went on. 'All a man can eat is one meal at a time. All he can love is one woman at a time. None of us has tomorrow; in fact, none of us has a minute beyond the present. You are going to die and so am I. Only perhaps, if the formula isn't broken, you should die sooner—you are older than I and you are sick.'

'Death comes suddenly—sometimes.'

Parker felt of that statement. Was there a warning in it? If there were danger in it, he could not find it.

André rode down the street on a dark horse. He lifted his hand and rode south. Parker watched him leave Elkhorn. In two hours, dawn would come in. He wasn't tired. He started to the hotel. Just then, he saw Hawkins ride out of the livery barn. Hawkins went down a side street, and Parker saw him join André on the edge of town. Why hadn't they ridden out together?

Parker went to the barn and got his own horse. He lifted his saddle up and let it down on the broad back. He threaded the latigo through the cinch-ring and pulled it tight and went up. He did not ride out the front door but went out the back and came to the hills. He pointed the bronc south.

But when he came to the ridge, when the hills and valley lay below him, he saw no sign of either Hawkins or André. He turned and looked hard to the east, but the moonlight showed no rider there, either. He was quiet in his saddle. Something was talking inside of his brain, warning him as this sense had warned him so many times before.

He saw the pair, then. They were moving west, heading in the general direction of the hills that held the big Heart Bar Six. They came into the folds of the hills and there Parker lost them. Well, their business was their own business.

He ran this thing around his mind. Luke Smith, a man he'd never seen, was dead; Smith had worked for dying Ike Savage, and therefore he had been killed. What had he known to drive some unknown person to murder?

Then there was the Sioux buck, Crazy Springs. He had died with a knife plunging into his back, pushing out his life. Why had he been killed? To silence him, that was all; to silence him so he wouldn't tell what he knew to Parker.

Parker rode ahead, still south. Two miles went by and he cut around the base of a hill. He reached this with his horse blowing hard, and found a clump of buckbrush. He left the breathing bronc there, took his rifle and worked back. He saw a horseman and he moved into the sandstones, dark and tall there in the moonlight. Dawn was pushing into the sky.

The rider came up and Parker let his muscles fall. He put his rifle under his arm and walked out. He said, 'Sheriff, you're off your range, aren't you?'

Sheriff Ed Jones had his saddle on a buckskin. He reached and looked at Parker. 'My range is this entire country, gambler,' he said.

Parker settled on his haunches. He laid the rifle across his thighs. 'Get down, Jones,' he said.

Jones stepped down and the buckskin stood with trailing reins. He came over and sat beside Parker.

'You followed me,' said Parker.

'Yes.'

'Why?'

'There's something big here. I'm getting into what it is. Every man on this range has my suspicions until this is over. Therefore you fell under my eyes.'

'Why?'

Jones drew a thumb through the ground. 'You're new, for one thing. Another is, I don't know you very well. If I'd known you for a year or so, I might eliminate you.'

'You miss nothing, sir?'

'I try not to.'

Parker watched the man's thumb move the earth. The sunrise kissed the hills with imaginary lips. He pushed his hand toward the south. 'Whose place is that, sir?'

'André's homestead.'

Parker got to his feet. 'I'm hungry,' he said. 'Let's ride into town.' He got his horse and headed north again, the sheriff riding with him. And Sheriff Ed Jones, save for the time he coughed, made no other sound and did not speak again.

CHAPTER FOURTEEN

Parker awoke in the late afternoon.

He bathed in the tin tub and dressed with immaculate care. He put on fresh linen and a grey suit, the legs of the pants going into the justin half-boots he had just polished. He spread his wallet out on the bed and counted his bills. He had close to a thousand there. Beats punching cows, he thought.

An hour later he went in the lobby, where he nodded at the clerk and went out on the street. Jones was still sitting in front of his office, and he lifted a slow hand, letting it fall of its own momentum. Parker nodded and went into the café. Millie was back in the kitchen and he walked in there.

'The cook is drunk again,' she said. 'Why can't you men folks leave the bottle alone?'

'Some can't; some can. I can.'

She brushed a stray hair from her forehead. 'I've noticed that about you, Parker. I've noticed you're a little different.'

'Not different, Millie. I'd say, maybe, sensible? No use wearing out your belly with vile drink. But this sounds like a sermon.'

She smiled. 'I wouldn't mind marrying you.'

'Oh, Lord,' he said.

'The trouble is, you're too popular with the women. Those Savage girls, they eat out of your hands. Especially Connie.'

Parker looked at her levelly. He was serious. 'Do you really mean that, Millie? Does it look that way?'

'From here, yes.'

Parker ate and went to the Double Diamond. The proprietor was counting his change with the bills and coins scattered around his desk. Parker glanced at the bills and then looked at one hard. It was a ten-dollar bill.

'I'll buy this off you,' he said.

The man looked up. 'I don't get your point.' He was a methodical man and he wanted an answer for every action. Parker took the bill without answering and gave the man one of his own ten-dollar bills, after looking at it carefully.

'Like the looks of this particular bill,' he said.

He went outside and went to his room. He was breathing a little heavily. He spread the bill out on the chair and went to his saddlebags and took out a magnifying glass. He put it on the bill and studied it for some time, tested the paper of it. The paper was good and the bill crackled as he snapped it.

He put the bill down again and put his little glass away. He got to his feet and walked up and down the room. Then he put the bill in his pocket and went to the bank. Trundell was at his desk and the clerk was at his. The banker himself came to the grilled window.

'Could I see you alone, Trundell?'

Trundell unbarred the waist door and took Parker into his office. The banker closed the door behind them. He showed Parker to a chair, but the gambler kept standing. Trundell went behind the big desk and sat down.

'What can I do for you?'

Parker handed him the ten-dollar bill. Trundell's forehead showed a set of fine wrinkles. Parker was playing a lone hand, a wolf hand. He watched the banker closely. Trundell turned the bill slowly in thin fingers. He tested it for strength and then lifted his glance to the gambler.

'Well?'

'Get a glass,' said Parker.

Trundell took a small glass from a drawer and laid it against the bill. He moved the glass up and down and got the proper focus. He was silent then, mouth drawn into thin lines, his forehead smooth. He let time run by before he lowered the glass and leaned back in his chair, fingers playing with the bill.

'What about this bill?'

Parker said, 'Counterfeit.'

'How can you tell?'

'I've handled lots of money. In fact, I might have handled more than you have, even though you work in a bank. I've grown to know the feel and crackle of a genuine piece of paper. I've even gone to school—a school for gamblers, mind you—and there I've found out the difference in sight and feel between good and bogus bills. This one is flat.' He pointed out slight variations in color and texture. Trundell listened, and Parker thought he saw surprise in the man's eyes.

'You know it,' said Trundell. 'Where did you get this?'

Parker told him.

'Wonder where the Double Diamond boss got it?'

Parker remembered something. He added two and two and he got four. He decided not to tell this to the banker.

'In this trade, I guess. Have you ever found a bum bill before in your bank receipts?'

Trundell thought. 'Three, so far. This is

108

the third, the one you have. We've found two in the bank, and this one. The first one was three years ago, before I came. I found one since I came.'

'How long ago?'

Trundell thought. 'A year, maybe. Might be less.'

The gambler was silent for ten seconds. He was trying to see how all this could fit in, and it didn't fit. Would it dovetail together later?

'Where do you fit in?'

Trundell asked, 'What do you mean?'

Parker sat down. 'Let's not fool around with words,' he said. 'I work for Ike Savage. Savage says there is something wrong on this range. I know there is, since Luke Smith and the Indian got killed. I won't mention some other things that happened—such as thugs jumping on me and beating me and threatening my life. But there is something rotten here. It stinks high.'

'Go on.'

'There are no more words. Where do you fit?'

Trundell's long fingers drummed on the desk. 'You talk straight, Parker; I like that. All right, I'll talk straight, too. I don't own this bank. When the old owner found that bill—that counterfeit bill—he sent it into the United States Treasury. I was there, and I came out and took over his bank while the old man went on a long vacation. It is still his bank. Most people think I bought it; I want them to think that.'

'Then you're a government man?'

'I am.'

'And you're after some counterfeiters?'

'That's right.'

Parker got to his feet. 'I'll keep this to myself, of course. Maybe we can work together, now that we both know this. Where do you think this counterfeiting nest is? Do you think it is around here?'

'I don't know.'

Parker studied him.

'These bills—bills of the same texture, same printing—have come out all over the United States. They've appeared mostly in the big Eastern cities. New York has had lots of them; so has Boston. This is a big ring. But somebody, we think, has slipped. And I'll tell you why. These bills have showed up strong in Seattle, Spokane, San Francisco and Los Angeles. None have showed in Denver and Salt Lake. But three now have come out in Elkhorn, Montana.'

Parker nodded. 'You think somebody around here has erred, huh? You got a hunch they're being produced around here and then going East for release, but three have accidentally seen light here?'

'We don't know; we just guess.'

Parker left, with Trundell showing him outside. Parker asked if Sheriff Ed Jones knew about these bills and Trundell said he had not notified the lawman. Parker went to his room and sat down. He kept out of line of the window. He leaned back in the chair, closed his eyes and thought. But the chair was too uncomfortable; he lay on the bed and let his thoughts take over.

He lay there for over an hour, then came awake as the door opened and Jetta Savage came in.

'Don't you ever knock?' he asked.

Her red hair lay in glistening coils down her shoulders in braids. As usual, her hat hung by the chin-strap. Her blouse was white silk and her skirt and jacket were of smooth buckskin. She sat down and crossed her legs, and Parker looked at her polished boots with their silver-inlaid spurs and star rowels. She caught his eye and smiled a little crookedly.

'I've got pretty legs, don't you think?'

Parker sat up on the edge of the bed, did not answer for some time. He knew that silence would make her nervous.

'Yes, you've got pretty legs. What are you doing here?'

'Just passing by. I thought I'd drop in.'

'You sure that's all?'

Her grey eyes were sharp. 'Well, I guess—'

Parker got to his feet. 'You'd better go,' he said. 'It doesn't look good in a small town for a pretty girl to come to a gambler's room. Gamblers are notorious for their use of

111

women, you know, and tongues will talk.'

She stood up. 'Let them talk.'

Parker took her by the shoulders and held her. He turned her hard, and at the same time he took the gun from her jacket pocket. He let her go and he looked at the gun. 'Why do you carry that?'

Her cheekbones stood out. She said, 'Give me that gun!' and grabbed. Parker moved the gun back, still holding it. She got hold of her nerves. She stood and bit her lip, and her eyes were savage.

'I could kill you!'

'Maybe you came to do just that?' Parker clipped the words.

She stared at him. Her tongue came out and wet her lips. 'Why would I kill you, you tinhorn?'

Was she fishing for information? She sounded as though she were. Parker spoke wearily. 'There's the door, Jetta. Use it. I'll get your gun back to you. Guns don't go good with a pretty girl like you.'

'Damn you,' she said.

She left. Parker heard her footsteps go down the stairs. Why had she come to visit him? Did she usually pack this gun? He rolled the gun in his hands and kicked out the shells. He tossed the bullets into the basket on the floor and put the gun in his pocket. Dusk was coming across the range.

He went downstairs. He didn't want to eat:

he felt a little sick at his stomach, the feeling that comes with disgust. Jetta's horse wasn't on the street. He got a cup of coffee at the café.

'You work long hours, Millie,' he said.

She was bright again, smiling. Parker caught a sudden glimpse of her womanhood, and he saw she was deep in character, with many facets. 'That cook sobered up a little, the devil. I got him back to work.'

Parker got a cup of coffee.

Men moved in and out of the café. Millie was busy and another girl took the booths. Parker nursed his coffee. The sick feeling was leaving him. He was ready to leave when Connie Savage came in and took the stool beside him.

'Your dad, Miss Connie?'

'The same, I guess.'

He handed the .32 to the girl. 'This belongs to your sister.'

CHAPTER FIFTEEN

Martin Trundell locked his bank and went home for supper. He let the night gather, then got his horse and rode out of Elkhorn. The wind was sighing through scrub pine on the ridges.

When he gained Hogback Ridge, he kept

113

his bronc still in the high buckbrush. A rider was toiling to the west, dark in the dim light of the rising moon. Trundell looked at the moon and wondered whether it would be a detriment or an asset. He decided on the latter. Come another week and the moon would be gone; there would be only darkness then, and a man couldn't do much in the dark.

Good old Ed Jones, he thought. Up to his old trick of trying to shadow Martin Trundell.

He ducked back and left the ridge, traveling east. He circled and came in behind Ed Jones, who still trailed south. There in the moonwashed sandstones, Martin Trundell watched the lawman lose his trail. Trundell grinned and looked back toward Elkhorn, hardly without wonder that nobody else trailed him. This night game of hide-and-seek among the hills was getting popular since Parker had come to this Montana range.

Trundell rode due west.

He rode for miles. The lupine was blue in the grass and he caught its clinging odor. He went west, always west. An hour slipped into eternity. He was over a small herd of cattle, Heart Bar Six cattle, that slept in a gully. Trundell watched them for ten minutes, then turned his horse. He held the animal sharply and listened. Below them, cattle were getting to their feet.

Then he saw the two riders who had brought the dogies up. They were too far away for identification; the night was too dim. They took the cattle to their feet, cut the herd in two, and put one half of them toward the valley. They ran them with their lass-ropes doubled to beat them across the back. Trundell did not stir from the brush. He had dismounted now and he had tied his bandanna around the jaws of his horse to keep him silent.

There was a man behind him on the ridge; he knew that for sure. The man was higher than Trundell, and that made him dangerous, for he could shoot down—could see him easier, too, although the buckbrush was much higher than a horse and rider where Trundell had hidden.

The banker settled on his thighs, cold and deadly inside. The two buckaroos who had hazed the cattle out were down on the basin floor now, heading them toward the fence section owned by a farmer. Trundell listened for another rock to roll down and show him where the hidden man was. He smiled ironically. Was that hidden man Ed Jones? He doubted that; Jones was far behind him, lost from his trail.

Trundell had his rifle beside him. His horse was tired; therefore the animal stood rock-still, head down. The banker was glad of that. He moved off to one side about a hundred feet, working his way carefully and with great deliberation. Finally he reached the point he wanted. Now let his bronc stomp if he wanted. The hidden rifleman would come in at the point where the horse stood, and Trundell would move in behind him.

He heard a blast to the east. The air shook and flame shot up. The blast was about four miles away. He saw cattle running wildly, madly. One of the riders had tossed a stick of dynamite behind the cattle. The explosion had thrown them into a wild stampede. They pounded toward the fence.

Trundell thought, Some farmer'll lose his field and his fence when them cattle smash across his land. He could see the moving shapes of the running cattle; then he lost sight of them. Now he saw the two riders coming back at a mad lope, heading for the rest of the cattle that had remained in the ravine. They came fast, circled the herd, beat the cows with lariats and headed them west, running them toward the high foothills.

Clouds were up, running across the face of the moon and again Trundell could not recognize the riders. He thought of working his way closer, but he knew that was out of the question. A few yards ahead the buckbrush thinned out, and they'd see him out there on that brushless strip. And besides, there was a man behind him.

He had no other choice but to sit and wait

until the herd was gone. Already the cattle were moving into the deep hills. The hills seemed to reach out and drag them in with their riders. Trundell waited until the herd had left his vision, waited another hour beyond that. He hunkered, and then he'd shift slightly to ease the strain on the muscles of his thigh.

Dawn was coming in. He watched it caress the hills, touch the brush, rub a magic paintbush across the pines and firs. He knew he would have to make a move soon. He hoped the guard had gone, but he couldn't afford to wait any longer. With full daylight close, the guard—if he were still up there—could make him and his horse out easily, for when daylight came this brush would be clear.

So the banker moved ahead. He was tight across the spine, for it isn't nice to expect a bullet to crash into your back at any moment and snap your life out of you. He moved ahead and upward, leaving his horse further behind. He would travel a way stooped over, would run hard. Then he would settle down and watch and wait and scout the brush ahead, looking for his path.

He got almost to the summit; so far, no bullets. He felt the wariness run out of him, leaving a tired feeling behind. But still he used vigilance. He moved ahead again for ten feet. Below him he saw his horse now; saw him clearly in the dawn. He stood up and moved ahead boldly.

Then the bullet came.

Trundell was aware of a pin suddenly pricking his shoulder. He stumbled and fell, and the second bullet went high, hit a rock. He thought, That was a rifle bullet—not a pin-point. A steel-jacketed rifle bullet that slipped right through my shoulder. My shoulder's numb.

He could feel his blood now. It was coming out of his shoulder, moving down his back and his chest. He got his rifle ahead of him and across a handy rock and he lifted the barrel. He saw a wisp of powdersmoke hanging over a boulder. He shot at it, and he heard his bullets slap across space after skipping from a boulder. He shot three times, then held fire with his finger crooked around the trigger. The sound of shooting died. Trundell was well hidden. A few minutes passed, and the banker felt a tinge of nausea, knew shock was setting in. He wanted to tend to his shoulder but he couldn't; not here nor at this time.

The sound of horse hoofs, pounding into the distance, came to him. That meant that the ambusher was leaving. The horse was running hard on the other side of the ridge, and the sound pulled out and died in the thin morning. Trundell figured there had only been one man, and he was correct. He gained the top of the ridge, breathing hard, but the rider was already out of sight.

Trundell smiled. He caught the irony of this: the town banker out trading shots with an unknown gunman over stolen Heart Bar Six cattle. Not his cattle, and bankers were supposed to look after their own property, nobody else's. He knelt there, sick and bloody, and looked down at his horse. The horse lay on his side. That rifleman's killed my horse, thought Trundell.

He did not remember hearing the shots that had killed his bronc, but things had been mixed up, after that bullet had dropped him. He was lucky the lead hadn't ripped through his heart. The bullet had come low on his shoulder, passing through the thick flesh between his arm and chest, right below the socket.

The banker shrugged to see if his shoulder blade were broken; it wasn't. He sat down and took out his pocket knife and cut off his shirt sleeve, cutting back into the body of the shirt. He threw this away, a bloody mess. He split his cotton undershirt and pulled it off him. Under his clothes he had a hard, muscular body. He used the undershirt for a bandage.

He had difficulty tying it into place, but finally got that done. He looked at his watch; it was after six. By this time, that stolen herd would be a long way off, and the hills over that way were really tough for trailing. He'd keep that to himself when he saw the sheriff; Ed Jones didn't need to know everything.

He went down the slope, taking his time. He didn't want to fall and slide in shale; he might break the congealed blood loose and start his shoulder bleeding. He reached his horse. The animal had been felled with a rifle bullet between his ears; he'd make no more midnight runs. Trundell felt a great anger. He liked horses, and this was his top bronc.

He had no other choice but to walk to the nearest farmhouse. He figured that the closest one belonged to Olaf Johnson, a Norwegian, and that it was at least five miles away. He headed out after leaving his spurs beside his dead horse. He still carried his rifle in his good hand.

★   ★   ★

Almost two hours later, he came across the field where Johnson was harrowing, dust rising behind his four-horse team. The farmer ran to the barn and harnessed a team to the democrat rig and came back, bouncing in the seat as the democrat lurched across the fresh ploughing.

'My wife, she'll help us.'

Mrs. Johnson was a big woman. Between herself and her slow-speaking husband, they got the banker on the seat. Trundell was almost spent; he had not known he was so all in. He let his head fall.

The woman had her heavy arm around him, holding him still. Trundell felt suddenly small and weak. 'I had my pistol out ready to shoot at a cotton-tail rabbit,' said the banker. 'Just for practice, you know. My horse fell and the gun went off—'

'Be quiet,' said the woman.

They reached the lane where the hard-packed wagon road ran into Elkhorn. Trundell saw the broken fence and the field horribly pounded down by cattle hoofs. Heart Bar Six cattle grazed on the ruined wheatfield.

'What happened?' he asked.

Olaf Johnson answered. 'There was a terrible roar last night. Cattle came running and they went through the fence. Now Harry Lynch's field is ruined and his fences are torn down. And his missus is sick in bed, too, and Harry has been ailing.'

'Wonder what stampeded the cattle?'

'There was a loud noise; then they ran.'

Trundell looked at the desolation. This would further incite the farmers against old Ike Savage and his Heart Bar Six men. Who had run this stock through here, and why? Was there an outside gang working on this range to cause trouble between the Heart Bar Six and the farmers?

The rest of the ride was made in silence.

Olaf Johnson stopped his rig in front of the doctor's office. The medico was just opening up. He and Sheriff Ed Jones helped Trundell down and into the office.

'What happened to you?' asked the sheriff.

Trundell felt sick. 'Olaf will tell you,' he said.

CHAPTER SIXTEEN

Parker was dressing when Jed Hawkins knocked at the door. The farmer was dusty and tired-looking. He told Parker about the stampeding Heart Bar Six cattle and how they had been terrified by a great noise.

'What caused the noise?'

Hawkins shrugged. 'Darned if I'd know. Accordin' to what I've heard, there was a big roar with plenty of fire and flame. These cattle came hell-bent-for-election on the run, wild with fear.'

'Dynamite, I wonder?'

'I sure don't know, Parker. Maybe it was one of these falling stars that hit the earth—you know, meteors. Ain't that what they call them things?'

Parker told him he was correct. According to what he had heard, that was possible—he'd read about meteors hitting the earth and causing flame and roar. He asked Hawkins how the farmers were taking it. The man's heavy face fell into thick lines. Some of the farmers claimed that the Heart Bar Six had stampeded their cattle over the fields, just to get the farmers mad.

'But I thought the Heart Bar Six was going to pull out,' said Parker.

Hawkins spread his hands suggestively. 'Sure, that's what Ike Savage says, of course. But Ike's flat on his back an' helpless. Them two hellion heifers of his are running the spread, and Kirt Stanton ain't no angel. He might tell ol' Ike one thing and do another; that's been done, you know.'

Parker smiled. 'Too many times,' he agreed.

The gambler finished dressing. Hawkins took a snort out of the bottle on the dresser that Parker kept for his visiting friends. The farmer watched Parker strap on the .32 in its spring-holster.

'Quite a rigging,' he allowed.

Parker said, 'It has come in handy.'

They went down the stairs together, an immaculate gambler and a farmer with riding boots and heavy spurs. 'That explosion, or whatever it was, woke me up last night,' stated Hawkins. 'Didn't get much sleep. I'm kinda droopy today.' He yawned.

'Hungry?'

'I could stand a mite to eat.'

Parker noticed that Ed Jones was missing

from the bench. Hawkins told him the lawman had ridden out to the scene of the stampede. A farmer was loading barbwire on his wagon, and Hawkins stopped and talked to him. Parker went on toward the café. He couldn't keep from hearing the loud tones used by the farmer who talked to Hawkins. He met Trundell, who had his left arm in a sling.

'What happened to you?'

Trundell told him that his horse had fallen where he had been shooting a cotton-tail, and they had both been shot. 'Only the cotton-tail got away,' said the banker. 'What a fool accident. Never have heard nothing like this, have you?'

Parker told him about a story he had heard about a cowpuncher who had bought an automatic .45. He was going to shoot at a coyote. His bronc grabbed for the horn and he pulled trigger accidentally, shooting his bronc through the back of the head and killing him.

'I did better than that,' said Trundell. 'I shot both myself and the bronc.'

Trundell went on down the street and Hawkins caught up with Parker. 'That hoeman was kinda hot under the collar,' he said. 'He wants action against the Heart Bar Six. I kind of got him quieted down some, I hope. We're holding another meeting in a day or two to talk this over.' He shook his head slowly. 'Jones better get this straightened up soon or else I can't keep these farmers down any longer. Hell'll rip loose if the sod-busters go on the warpath.'

'Where do you think Jones stands?'

Hawkins looked at him. He did not answer right away. 'I don't know for sure. Who knows where anybody stands on this graze?'

When Parker went down on the street that evening, a fiddle was scraping in the distance, and with it were the sounds of a harmonica and a banjo. The dance was getting under way at the schoolhouse. Here in the cow country the only big entertainment was the weekly dances. At these men and women gathered and talked while children ran and played until tired. Then the kids were bedded down in straw and hay, packed in the beds of buggies and wagons to sleep until their parents went home, usually in the grey dawn.

It was too early to start his table running, so Parker walked to the schoolhouse. Benches and desks had been pushed aside against the wall where already people sat on them. A few couples were dancing a slow waltz. Parker watched for a little while, then went to the Double Diamond. Some farmers and a few Heart Bar Six cowboys. He noticed the fat proprietor seemed worried. Parker ordered a lemonade and sipped it slowly. The proprietor moved back and forth, tending to the wants of his customers.

'Getting another bartender on,' he said. 'This will be a big night.'

'Trouble?'

'Sure hope not.'

Parker sipped his lemonade. 'I want to leave about twelve,' he said; 'want to get to the dance. You'll have a man over at my table to take over?'

'All right, Parker.'

Parker thanked him and finished his lemonade. He walked to the back room and carefully washed his hands. He scrubbed them with a small stiff brush in the warm water and rubbed them on a thick towel. He bent his fingers and straightened them out. He did not relish this night of cards, and wondered why.

He went to his table and hung up his sign. The game ran back and forth, and he found himself thinking of that bogus ten-dollar bill he had collected in one of these games. Who had handed it to him? He kept running that thought around in his mind, but he could not find a definite answer. The choice seemed to fall between two men.

Hawkins bought chips. So did a Heart Bar Six cowboy called Mack. The cowboy was half drunk, and when he drank he grew angry. He was a short man. He had a run of hard luck, and Parker saw this angered him. Midnight finally came, and the cowboy was in a month's wages.

126

A tall gambler came over and said, 'That time, Parker,' and Parker let him have the chair. The cowboy growled something about quitting when ahead, and Parker looked at him steadily. 'Trouble with you?' he asked.

The cowboy had his bluff called. His eyes burned hard and held that way, and then he shrugged.

Hawkins looked up, 'See you at the dance, Parker.'

Parker nodded and went to the bar. He counted out the currency and bills, and found himself studying the paper money. He caught Hawkins glancing at him; the farmer returned to his cards. The gambler got his cut and put it in his wallet and walked outside. The moon was just lifting over the ridges. The odor of pine pitch and green grass was in the cool air. Parker walked slowly down the street. The clean air out here was a contrast to the smoke-filled atmosphere of the Double Diamond.

He went to the livery barn. Connie Savage sat on the bench and talked with the old hostler. The old man, as usual, was under the influence of John Barleycorn, and Connie had a good start herself.

She offered the quart bottle to Parker. 'Thanks,' he said. 'Not tonight, though.' He felt disgusted. She seemed helpless, without character, and he had a sudden pity for her. He had the swift impression that something was driving her—something hidden, something bitter, something he could not see or did not understand. He was sure of that.

He got his horse and rode out.

CHAPTER SEVENTEEN

Parker came in from the south and tied his horse a mile back of the big Heart Bar Six Ranch. He was taking no chances of being seen this time. He went through the buckbrush and wild rosebushes toward the ranch house. His nostrils caught the sweet scent of wild roses and sweet peas.

He did not go directly to the house but circled and stopped in the brush opposite the cabin occupied by Kirt Stanton. There was a kerosene lamp lighted in the range boss' shack. Parker let his mind dwell for a long second on this man. Again he decided that Stanton was no leader; he was a follower. But the man loved Jetta Savage. And Jetta would lead him where she wanted; in his weakness lay the man's strength and his danger.

A light showed in Jetta's cabin, too, but Connie's cabin was dark. Suddenly Parker remembered Connie down in the barn: he remembered her sudden, appealing glance. Then the rock hardness had come in and blotted that out. But he had glimpsed it and he had wondered about it.

The back door was unlocked. He went down the hall, the stink of the lupine in his nostrils. Ike Savage's door was closed. He knocked softly and told his identity. Savage said, 'Come in.'

The lamp was wicked low, Savage's silvery hair reflected the light and the shadows fell across his sullen, wrinkled face. He took his hand out from under the covers, taking the .45 with it. He laid the gun beside him.

'You won't need that,' said Parker.

'What have you got to say?'

'Who is taking care of you?'

'An old man on the ranch. He takes care of the saddle stock in the barn. Why do you ask?'

'Just curious, that's all.'

Savage closed his eyes.

Parker said, 'Trundell got shot. He claims he got shot in an accident, but I don't believe it. I don't know which side of the fence he is on: he might be astraddle it or on our side or against us.'

'You think that will is causing this?'

Parker rubbed his jaw. 'It might be that. Yes, I believe that is part of it. But I can't help feeling there's something bigger behind it, something we can't see. Trundell is after bigger game—he says.' He told Savage about the bogus ten-dollar bill, also told him about the placard that he had found on himself after the squat man and another had jumped him.

'Maybe that humpback was Crazy Springs,' said Savage.

'I've thought of that. But I don't think so.'

'There should be another clue soon,' said Savage.

Parker asked, 'You have a cowpuncher working for you named Mack. He was at my table down in town tonight. He's a poor poker player; didn't like the way I treated him. He works for you?'

'Yes.'

'He and Jed Hawkins seem friendly.'

Savage's bright eyes were on him. 'What do you see in that?'

Parker thought. 'I don't know. Maybe nothing.'

'Is Ed Jones dead yet?'

'No.'

Savage closed his eyes again. 'I hope he will be soon. I want to outlive that dirty dog. We never did get along. I hope he's wrapped up in this and that he stops lead with his guts. But I don't think he is; he's too ignorant and too bull-headed.'

*　　　*　　　*

Parker thought of the grey horse and rider in the snowstorm. Maybe Sheriff Jones was tied up in this. Savage kept his eyes closed. Gradually his hand pulled back. He dragged

130

the heavy .45 across the quilt, and the claw and gun ducked under the cover and went down again. The hand finally stopped. The gun and his hand made a bump under the quilt. The covers rose a little, falling to the man's shallow breathing. The mouth came open a little, the lips receded over toothless gums, and the old cowman slept.

Parker stepped out into the night, and then he pulled back under the shadows, looking around.

But he read no danger in the stillness.

He went ahead into the brush. Thirty feet from the house, he heard the sudden crack of a twig under a boot. He settled down immediately, crouching in the brush. The bullet beat over him and another followed.

Parker never knew where the bullets finally landed. Only knew that his sudden movement had saved his life. He had his .32 out and up. He emptied the little gun, put a square of bullets around the spot where the gun had spoken.

He heard a man gasp. A body hit the ground. The roar was bringing men out of the bunkhouse. They came running out, hanging on to their guns. The place was in an uproar. He heard Kirt Stanton hollering.

'Back of the house,' somebody said.

Parker wondered whom he had shot. He had two outs: one was to run for his horse, find saddle, and ride out—and probably have the Heart Bar Six men trailing him with rifles: the other was to duck back into Ike Savage's room. He did this.

Savage asked, 'What happened?'

'A man jumped me. I dropped him.'

'Who was he?'

'I don't know.'

'Where's your horse?'

'Back in the brush. A long way back. Over a mile back, I'd say.'

'They'll never find him, never go back that far. Get in that closet there. Hurry, Parker.'

The gambler went into the clothes closet, closed the door solidly and hunkered, looking out the keyhole. He could see Ike Savage's bed. The old cowman lay back again, and Parker could see the bulge of the .45 under the covers.

Outside, men were moving. Finally Kirt Stanton came into the room. Savage said angrily, 'Ain't you got sense enough to knock at a man's door?'

Stanton did not answer that. 'There was some shooting outside,' he said. 'Mack got killed. Somebody shot him to death.'

Parker heard each word. He felt a sense of wonderment. The cowboy must've trailed him out from town and lain in wait. But why?

'Who killed him?'

Stanton said, 'We don't know.'

'Good riddance,' said Savage.

Stanton stood silent. He seemed

132

undetermined. Finally he asked, 'You ain't heard nobody come into the house to hide, have you?'

'No.'

'Maybe we better search the house.'

'Go ahead, if you want to. I heard the shots; I didn't hear a man enter the house until you came. But search if you care to. Get out of my room now; I don't like your looks this late at night.'

Stanton left.

Parker heard men moving throughout the house, heard doors bang. This went on for ten minutes. He was restless, penned in the small room. Finally the house grew quiet. The yard grew quiet, too. Parker came out of the closet.

'You'd better go,' said Savage.

Again Parker went down the hall and outside. This time no gun challenged him as he went through the brush. The entire ranch was dark save for the light in Ike Savage's window. The place had settled down.

Still the gambler was wary.

He had promised to meet Millie at two at the dance. It was almost that hour when he rode into the livery. Neither Connie nor the old man was around. He racked his horse, peeled leather from him, and went to his room. He washed and straightened his tie and brushed his suit and then went to the schoolhouse.

The town proper was silent. Occasional lights shone from saloons where late gambling went on. The Double Diamond was closed and dark. Only the schoolhouse, set on the west edge of town, showed any signs of life. The sound of the harmonica and violin grew stronger as he came closer.

Horses were tied to hitchracks and posts. A group of men stood by the door with a bottle here and there; cigarette coals glistened in the dark as their owners sucked in on them. The door was open and light streamed out, glistening on the hard, boot-pounded earth in front of the door.

Parker stepped around some horses. Suddenly he stopped and looked at one horse. He was a big horse, an iron-grey, and first he thought he was Sheriff Ed Jones' horse. Then he noticed there were no dark markings across his rump. But outside of that he was a dead ringer for the other bronc.

Parker watched him. 'Who owns that horse?' he asked a man.

'I don't know.'

Parker said, 'Nice-looking horse,' and went into the building.

CHAPTER EIGHTEEN

Sheriff Ed Jones was sitting on a bench inside the hall. He looked up at Parker and nodded. Jones was tired. He ached in every joint.

He sat there for thirty minutes, watching the dancers. He got to his feet and went outside. A man offered him a drink. He declined. Whisky just helped the bugs along, he told the man; and they didn't need any help. He smiled and went toward the main section of the town.

A rider came out of the night. 'Sheriff?'

'Here.'

The rider was Kirt Stanton. He leaned low in his saddle. 'Somebody's killed Mack,' he said. 'I got his body in front of your office.'

Stanton got off his horse and walked beside the sheriff, leading his animal. He told the lawman all he knew. 'Somebody was saying to me that Mack had been playing cards with this tinhorn and they didn't get along so well.'

'You mean Parker?'

'Yeah, him.'

'Parker's down at the dance now. He's with Millie Williams. He left the Double Diamond early, went to his room and had a nap, cleaned up and went to the dance. I seen a light in his room all the time.'

'I see.'

The horse stood with dragging hackamore rope. Stanton had tied the dead man securely and Jones had difficulty untying his share of the knots. His fingers didn't have the strength they used to have. They got the man loose and carried him into the office and laid him on the bench. He was pretty bloody.

'Whoever shot him didn't miss, looks like.' Jones rubbed his hands together to get some heat into them. 'Looks like he got shot with a small-bore gun, too. What're you telling, me, Stanton? The guy got killed by the back door of the ranch? You aren't stuffing me, are you?'

'Murder's a serious thing,' growled Stanton. 'You think one of us—either me or my men—murdered him? Are you hintin' at that?'

Jones smiled a little. 'Don't jump to conclusions.'

They went to the barn where the sheriff saddled his iron-grey horse. The lawman sent a quick glance around, noticing that no horses were missing from stalls. He got his oxbow and went up, and he and Stanton rode toward the Heart Bar Six.

'No use in going fast,' said Jones. 'We can't see nothing anyway until the sun comes up, which will be an hour or so.'

The jolting of the horse made Jones' bones ache harder. Stanton rode deep in saddle, taciturn and gruff.

'There's a lot of trouble here,' he said suddenly. 'Fences cut and cattle stampeded, Crazy Springs murdered, Luke Smith killed—or do you figure Luke committed suicide?'

'I guess he got killed.'

'Who do you figure killed him?'

Jones had no answer to that.

*　　*　　*

They rode past bunches of Heart Bar Six cattle. Jones noticed that all Savage stock had been driven from Muleshoe Basin. The cows were all back in the hills. Stanton had line-riders along the rim of the valley, and they met one at Buggy Springs. Stanton talked to one of them and then loped up to catch Jones again.

'Talked with Slim Jergens. Slim never seen no off-trail riders out this way. This killing of Mack kinda unnerves me. None of us are safe, I guess.'

Jones grunted.

Cowpunchers were having breakfast when they came into the Heart Bar Six. Jones and Stanton ate. Stanton had asked the lawman if he wanted to see the place where Mack had been killed, but the sheriff said he was hungry and wanted to eat first. He sat and looked out the window at the bedroom where

137

Ike Savage lay.

Stanton finished eating. He went out, and Jones heard him giving orders to his riders. Somewhere a bronc squealed as a rope settled on him. A horse started bucking and Jones watched through the open door. The cowpuncher put up a good ride and got the horse turning, and then he and another man loped out of sight over the hill. Stanton came back in and Jones shoved away his empty coffee cup.

'You coming?' asked Stanton.

'After more coffee.'

Stanton scowled and went outside. The Chinese cook filled the coffee cup again. Jones nursed it along and let the sun come up. He got to his feet, thanked the cook, and went back of the ranchhouse. Evidently Ike Savage saw him through the window. He called to him.

Jones asked, 'You want to see me, Savage?'

'I called your name, didn't I?'

Jones went down the hall and into the room. He took off his hat and held it between his fingers. Savage was just finishing breakfast. Jones wondered how a man could eat with that lupine odor around him.

'Put your hat back on,' growled Savage. 'You're not at my funeral yet.'

Jones put on his hat.

'You've come out to look and see where Mack got shot up, huh?' Savage did not wait

138

for an answer. 'I don't think much of you as a lawman, Jones. I don't think you'll find out much.'

'The taxpayers must like me,' Jones replied civilly. 'They've elected me three terms in a row now.'

'Got to keep you off the county poor fund,' said Savage. 'If they hadn't elected you sheriff, they'd've had to support you by public funds. All right, mister, look away. If you find anything, let me know. But you won't find anything.'

Jones said, 'Thanks,' and his voice was dry.

The lawman went down the hall.

Connie Savage rode into the yard. She looked at Jones. 'Dad will love you being here,' she said ironically.

'You're drunk.'

'You don't say.' She rode into the barn.

Stanton found Jones behind the house. Jones said, 'I can read sign,' and Stanton went a little red. He stood there and then walked off. Jones picked up sign and followed it to where Parker had tied his horse. The horse tracks told him nothing; just another horse. He back-tracked and followed Mack's tracks. These also told him nothing. This was like a top that kept on spinning. It went around and around and had no answer. Jones felt the aching set in again.

He got his horse. Stanton came over and

asked, 'What do you say, Sheriff?'

'Good day,' said Jones.

Stanton watched him ride away.

Jones went due west, then, once out of sight, turned south. He went to where he had seen the prints of Parker's horse. He cut this sign and followed it and then lost it on the flat. The tracks had been running toward town. He didn't care much who had killed Mack. The cowboy, he figured, wasn't much count, anyway. But he would like to know why he had been killed.

Jones came into town in the early forenoon. He went to the café and ordered some coffee. The town was dull and lifeless, sleeping after its Saturday night. Millie looked tired.

'You don't get enough sleep,' said Jones.

'Neither do you,' she countered.

Jones smiled and nursed his coffee along. He watched a devil-twist of wind move sharply down the dust of the main street. It ran fast and quick, lifting the dust in a funnel; then suddenly it broke and expired. The dust dropped and fell and was without movement. Jones thought, A man's a lot like that. He walks his days and makes a big stir about little things that don't matter.

'How was the dance, Millie?'

'I had a good time.' She was serious. 'Everybody knows about Mack being killed; everybody is wondering. Some are afraid.'

'I suppose so.'

140

She looked out the window. 'There goes Banker Trundell,' she said. 'The doctor said his shoulder healed awful fast. He sure was lucky to get off with such an easy accident. He could've been killed.'

Jones watched the banker ride out. He noticed Trundell packed a rifle in his saddle-boot and he had a .45. Trundell rode south. Jones took his attention from him and put it on his coffee.

'Wonder where he's going?' asked Millie.

Jones smiled. 'You women. All the same, always inquisitive. Well, I'd say he was going out to look at some farmer's property. Somebody probably wants to borrow money from the bank, and he might be going to look at his security.'

Millie nodded.

Jones finished his coffee and went outside. He took the bench in front of his office. After a while the hardware man and his gangling son came and took Mack's body. They carried the man into their store and into the back where they had some coffins stacked along the wall of the storeroom.

CHAPTER NINETEEN

Trundell rode at a running walk, holding his horse back a little. He wanted to enjoy the summer day. Meadowlarks sang and curlews stood along the creek, long beaks extended. One curlew put his beak deep into a crack in the earth and came out with a beetle. The banker watched the bird eat the insect.

The sun was beginning to be warm. He took off his flat-brimmed, black hat and fanned himself with it. An hour later, he rode into the farm, looking it over with a seemingly casual glance as he came through the open gate.

A dog came rushing out, barking. Trundell snapped his quirt, making the thongs pop. The dog scampered out of reach and stood silent. A man came out of the barn carrying a manure fork. He was a stocky fellow and he wore bib overalls, a blue denim shirt, and heavy brogans.

'Howdy, Trundell.'

Trundell nodded. 'Good day, sir.'

'You just look around,' the man said. 'I got some stalls to clean out. I'll be with you come ten, fifteen minutes.'

The farmer went back into the barn. Trundell came down and tied his horse to a post. The dog came up, wagging his tail. Trundell stopped and scratched the dog's head. The animal danced ahead.

First Trundell looked over the house. He walked all through it, taking his time. He looked at the floors, pounded the walls. He saw a ten-dollar bill on the bureau, glanced at it, then walked by. Suddenly he turned and looked at the bill. He left it lying there and he looked at it for a full minute.

He glanced around, took the bill and crackled it, listening very carefully to its sound. He held it up to the light and studied it.

He got a ten-dollar bill from his pocket and put it in the spot where this one had been, then rolled the bill carefully and put it in his pocket. He went on inspecting the house, but his heart was pounding hard—too hard, he thought.

The banker went outside, looked at the barn and the granary and the machinery. When the farmer left the barn, the banker sat on the steps of the porch, scratching the dog.

'How much do you need?' asked Trundell.

'Two thousand.'

Trundell nodded. 'I've got that on me. I've got the form for a promissory note, too. Let's go inside.'

They went into the living-room. 'The place is dirty,' said the man. 'My mother is comin' out from New York next month, I guess. Tough to have to work hard at farmin' an' to batch, too.'

'That's what I'd think, too.'

The farmer got pen and ink from the bureau drawer. Trundell looked at the ten dollars he had put there. 'Shouldn't leave money lying around,' he said.

The farmer put it in his pocket.

Trundell noticed that he had not glanced at the bill. He thought of the original ten-dollar note—the counterfeit one that had been on the bureau.

'Never noticed I had left it there,' said the farmer.

Trundell's heart had settled to its old rhythm. He spread the legal-looking paper on the table. The farmer read it at great length and Trundell waited patiently. Then the man said, 'All right, Trundell. Fill it out for two thousand.'

The banker filled in the form and handed the man the money which he counted from the roll in his pocket. He made two copies of the note, leaving one with the farmer. He got to his feet.

'Got a little riding to do yet,' he said. 'I hope you have much success, Mr. Watson. This valley has great farming potentialities.'

'Yeah, if the Heart Bar Six would only straighten out.'

Trundell got on his horse. He looked down at the dog who dozed in the shadows of the house. 'Perhaps that will happen,' he said.

The banker rode off at a long lope, put his horse into the hills. Once out of sight, he reined in and turned his animal, climbing a long ridge that ran out into Muleshoe Basin. Here he put his bronc in heavy underbrush and dismounted. He went to the lip of the

144

ravine and watched the basin below, settled under an igneous boulder.

Overhead an eagle wheeled. Trundell idly watched its shadow creep across the range. The sun was warm and it was hot in the shade. He loosened his necktie and let the air come into his collar. He felt better then; not so hot. From here he could see this southern end of the basin. Trails and fences and houses and fields were clear below him. From here he could see the house he had just left.

Watson left the house, went to the barn, and stayed there for some time, then returned to the house. The sun lifted and hung and started to fall. Still, Trundell waited. He got the ten-dollar bill from his pocket. He studied it again and saw he had been correct: it was a counterfeit and a good imitation.

Dusk came down. The eagle drifted back toward the mountains. A nighthawk whipped across the falling darkness, chasing flies and insects. Trundell let his nerves relax. He was too tight.

He let his head fall forward and he rested for a long moment, his eyes closed. He raised his head, and his eyes fell on the rider who moved out of Watson's farm. He was on an iron-grey gelding. First, Trundell thought it was Sheriff Ed Jones' horse; then, he noticed, through his field-glasses, that the beast lacked the rump markings of Jones' cayuse.

He put the glasses on the rider. 'Watson,'

the banker murmured. Watson was driving south, cutting across the huge talus cone at the base of this butte. Trundell wondered where the farmer was going. Well, he sure wasn't going toward Elkhorn.

Trundell got to his horse, found the stirrup and turned the beast, following the raw lip of the mesa. He was wary now: he was limber in leather; he was a manhunter. There was a joy to this game, none to waiting. He slid down a shale bed; the horse braced, and he came to a draw. He rode west in this, wariness still in his nerves, and came to a trail. A horse had passed over it recently, heading south—a lone horse, shod, and therefore a saddle horse.

Trundell knelt and looked south, in the direction of the tracks. He would not follow that trail. He moved straight west, came to Elk Creek, followed it. He went south now.

The brush was thick along the creek. He followed no trail. He had lost sight of his quarry, but that did not bother him. Had the man cut west, he'd hit his tracks. Once he saw him ahead, a mile or so. And Watson was still riding south.

But Trundell didn't like brush. He pulled his horse further west, intending to go to the hills. On the rim of the buckbrush, something smashed near him out of the saddle. He fell to the ground. He heard the sharp crack, of a rifle again. His horse stumbled and fell, lay silent.

Trundell was crawling toward the brush, five feet away. Another rifle bullet hit his thigh. He used his bum hand, scrambling. Blood was on his back and belly. He got to the brush and it and the darkness hid him.

He was giddy and the world turned around him. He got in the creek. He had ridden into an ambush, and Watson had set it, he knew. He wondered just where Watson was. Up there on that ridge somewhere.

He had his six-shooter, but his rifle lay back on his horse. He needed a rifle, too. He lay down in the water, felt it cut across his back and belly, taking the warm feeling away. The water below him was bloody in the dusk.

He had to get away; he was in no condition to make a fight out of it. All the odds were with his ambusher. He climbed out of the water, and his gun fell into the pool.

He heard a man coming.

Trundell waited, hidden, sick. The man walked by. It was Watson, sure enough. Trundell saw it all then. He had fallen for a ruse. That ten-dollar bill—that bum one—had been the bait.

All was clear to him now, too late. Watson had not wanted a loan, he had wanted him to see that bill. Watson was a part of this counterfeiting outfit—but who were the others?

Watson walked by, not more than twenty feet away. Had he had his six-shooter, he could have killed the farmer, had he strength enough to lift the heavy gun. And Trundell doubted that. His strength was running out of him, running down his back and his belly. Each second he lost more of it.

Suddenly he was desperate. He got up, fell down, landed on his hands and knees. There was a trail across the brush. He started creeping through it. He waded through a marsh, wallowing on hands and knees in the mud. He crossed it. He wondered if he were still bleeding. Did he have any blood left?

He sat against a rock. The trail was ten feet away. He wondered where Watson was. He could not hear the man; evidently he had gone in the other direction. Giddiness swept across him, spinning his brain like a mad top. He thought of trying to stop his blood from flowing out of him.

But he couldn't; he was doomed, and he knew it. Overhead a woodpecker drummed at a hollow limb. The noise sounded like somebody knocking at the door.

'Come in,' murmured Trundell.

Still the woodpecker knocked.

The banker thought of Parker. Parker was on this trail, too. How could he warn him? He took his hat and looked at it stupidly. Funny, he'd hung on to his hat all this time.

All this time . . .

He had a pencil in his shirt pocket. It was bloody. He felt around the inside of his hat's sweatband and came out with a line of paper he had used for packing to make the hat fit. He unrolled this and put it on his hat, using the flat brim to write on. He wrote slowly. He could barely see his words in the darkness.

Parker,
    Watson killed me. He had bill—rode south—he shot me from horse. He knows all about—
                M.T.

He couldn't sign his name; he was too tired. So he scrawled his initials. But he had to get the note in the trail. He crept to the ribbon of dust, got a small rock and placed the note down and put the rock over it to hold it.

That's done, he thought. I lived through that.

He had to get as far from the note as possible. He went back to the creek, creeping. He got in the water. It rushed him along and he found himself on the bank. Ferns and rushes were high here, and he crawled through them. He could not hear the woodpecker, only the babble of the creek.

He lay down, head on his arm. There was no pain now. He thought, I'm going to die,

149

and remembered he had often wondered what this moment would be like. He had once been afraid of this moment; now he welcomed it.

The sound of the creek stopped.

Out on the trail, a mile back in the hills, the wind fluttered a piece of paper. The rock hung on to it, sitting on one corner. The wind fluttered it again. The rock held on, then let loose. The wind caught the paper.

The wind pushed it into the brush. Ten feet off the trail, it caught and held on the root of a wild rosebush.

Nobody ever found it.

CHAPTER TWENTY

Parker looked at Ed Jones. 'Where's the banker?' he asked.

Jones looked at the bank. 'Blinds are down again today,' he said thoughtfully. 'They were down yesterday, too, and he didn't show up to open the bank. Do you suppose something's happened to him?'

Parker looked at him. 'Like what?'

'You guess,' said Jones testily. 'You seem good at guesses.'

Parker smiled a little.

'I wouldn't know,' he said.

He did some investigating. He went to Trundell's house; nobody was at home. The dog was whining and he let him outside. Jones came along. Parker said, 'His house was open. I let the dog out; he's hungry.'

'Where is he?' wondered Jones.

Finally the rest of the town started talking about it. Jed Hawkins sat on the porch in front of the hotel. 'Bet that gent took some of the bank's money—or all of it and jumped the country. I never did like him. Talked with a farmer yesterday, and he said he saw him riding north last Sunday.'

'Might be.'

Parker got his horse that morning and rode into the southern foothills. He was wary and missed nothing. He knew now that Trundell was dead; he had been killed.

He rode the ridges always. And he'd stop for hours in deep brush and look at the country below. He found no trace of either Trundell or his horse. Ed Jones was out riding, too, and the sheriff also was up against a blank wall.

Parker had gone far south on this day. He had seen André's homestead in the gulch, had seen the stooped man move between barn and house doing chores. Parker was doing a lot of thinking. There were a few items in his mind, hazy and dim, yet connected. One little clue would make their relation clear to him, he knew. The grey horse was one. At the dance, he had finally found out that the grey horse belonged to a farmer named Watson. Parker had seen the man and heard him talk at the farmers' meeting.

Watson had seemed an inoffensive, rather stupid fellow.

He had asked the hoemen to keep peace, not to move against the Heart Bar Six. Surely he had not ridden the horse—Parker put that aside. That grey horse had hard rump markings while Watson's horse—And why would a farmer kill another farmer?

When dusk came Parker was high on the rimrock. He was hunkered on his hams in the brush, watching the basin below turn dark. He kept thinking about Watson's grey horse. He saw the light go on in the farmer's house three miles or so away.

★   ★   ★

Darkness finally came. Parker got in saddle and rode toward that light. He left his horse in the buckbrush a quarter-mile away and went to the house on foot. He went into the barn through a feed window. From the doorway he could see Watson's house. The door was open and the dog lay inside the screen door, and beyond him Parker saw Watson moving back and forth, cooking supper. He caught the good odor of boiling ham and beans and realized he was hungry.

While he was watching, Watson came and shut the door, leaving the dog inside. Parker was glad he had not turned the dog outside. Slowly the gambler shut the door to the barn. Three horses were inside with the milch cow. Two of the horses were black horses: work horses. The other was the grey horse.

Parker lighted a match. He looked at the grey until the stick burned down and he had to drop it. He put his hand on the horse's shoulder and stroked him. The animal turned and nudged him with his nose, evidently begging for sugar.

'Sorry, old fellow,' murmured Parker.

The bronc was tame enough. The gambler ran his hand across the bronc's wide rump, petting him. The horse resumed eating hay from the manger. Parker stroked the base of the animal's tail. He lighted another match and looked at the horse's rump. All grey, with no dark markings.

He rubbed the hair back. Another match flared and he looked at the skin. He rubbed his finger along the roots of the hair and the match died. Parker went outside. He got to the brush, hunkered and lit another match, and looked at his finger. There was a dark rim of ink around it.

He had found his grey horse.

The gambler sat there and thought this over with puzzlement written across his face. He gave up. He rode into town, riding slowly. The old hostler looked at him from watery eyes and said, 'For a gambler, fellow, you sit a lot of saddle.'

'Good exercise.'

'I'll take mine in chair . . . with a bottle.'

Well, he'd found the grey horse.

He went to his room and lighted the lamp. Again he looked at his grimy finger. Looked like printer's ink, he thought. Printing made him remember the placard that had been left with him after they'd beat him up. There was a tie-up here. He knew it.

The hours passed slowly that night. Shortly after midnight, he closed his game. Sheriff Ed Jones stood beside the door. Parker asked him if he wanted to take a walk with him.

Jones asked, 'Afraid to go home alone?'

Parker smiled.

They reached the hotel, where they sat in the lobby and talked. Naturally their talk swung to the missing banker. Jones allowed that Trundell must've jumped the country with some dinero. Parker admitted that this might be true.

'Why don't you open his bank tomorrow?' asked the gambler.

Jones scowled and rubbed his hands together. 'We'll do that, huh? You know something about books, don't you?'

'A little.'

'We'll run through his books and see if they balance. I've got a key to the place; I got a key to every business house in town.'

Parker climbed the stairs to his room. He

had the blind low and the chair jacked against the door. He couldn't sleep. He lay with his hands clasped behind his head and he looked into the darkness. Toward morning a broken sleep finally came. He awoke at seven and shaved and went to the café.

Millie Williams had worked late and wouldn't be on shift until noon. Parker felt a little tired. She was the only bright, clean spot on this dirty range of intrigue and death.

Jones came in and ordered coffee. 'Trundell ain't in town yet,' he said. 'Maybe we'd better look into his bank, like we agreed.'

Parker nodded.

Jones was silent, lines drawn. 'This don't look good for me, Parker. Men disappearing from town; men getting killed. I wish I hadn't run for office the last time. A sick man ain't got no right to tote a star.'

Parker had no answer.

Before going to the bank, they went to Martin Trundell's home. The place was empty. One of the local kids had taken the dog to his home. Parker and the sheriff went through the place very carefully. Neither knew what he was really looking for, and they found nothing to tell them of Trundell's whereabouts. Parker was sure the man had a badland grave, but he did not tell this to Sheriff Ed Jones.

They went to the bank.

They came in by the rear door. The air was cool inside, with the blinds drawn, and the place had a closed, musty odor.

Jones coughed a little. 'It's chilly in here. What do you know about these books?' He shoved one at Parker.

Parker looked at its fly page. 'That's two years old.'

Jones got some more from a shelf. Parker found the current volume. He knew something about figures, and he quickly ran through the totals. The books looked all right, he told Jones. He went to the safe. It was locked. He twirled the dial absently.

Jones said, 'I know that combination. Trundell showed it to me one day. You know, he said that if something happened to him, he wanted me to know how to open that safe. He was an odd fellow.'

'He was a government man,' said Parker.

Jones was hunkered in front of the safe. He looked up at the gambler. 'What do you mean?'

'There's more than cow stealing on this range, Jones. Cow rustling is just one part of it, a small part. The rest is counterfeiting. Trundell came out here, posing as a banker, but really to track down these counterfeiters. Didn't you know that?'

Jones looked at him hard. 'No,' he finally said. He added, 'And why didn't he tell me, me being the law?'

'Wanted to work it quiet, I guess.'

Jones dropped his glance to the floor. Suddenly Parker wished he knew what the man was thinking. 'Well, I'll be doggoned. And what are you? A gover'ment man, too?' He lifted his gaze again.

'Just a gambler.'

'But you fit in somewhere—'

'Ike Savage,' explained Parker. 'Savage hired me to clean up his cattle range.' He decided to tell the sheriff everything he knew, but he did not tell him of the grey horse now at Watson's. Jones got to his feet, his eyes still wide. Parker knew then that the man was genuinely surprised. Jones did not have the mentality to put on such a convincing act.

'Are the Savage girls in on this?'

Parker lied. 'I don't think so.'

Jones turned the dial slowly. After four attempts he got the safe open. Parker settled beside him and saw the roll of bills and flat bills inside. Jones got to his feet.

'Well, he never rifled the bank an' pulled out. There's plenty of cash in there. They've killed him, Parker, or run him out of the country.'

Parker shook his head. 'Trundell wouldn't run.'

Jones said, 'I'm going to look around again.'

Parker still knelt beside the safe. There were papers there and some envelopes.

Evidently valuable papers and letters pertaining to the bank's affairs. Parker ran his thumb idly up and down a sheaf of currency.

Jones stopped. 'What's this, Parker?'

Parker crossed the room. The sheriff was looking at a letter. Parker read it and said, 'Only something about a mortgage, reads like.' He handed the letter back to Ed Jones. Jones put it back in its envelope.

Parker went back to the safe. There he found a sealed envelope with his name written on it in Trundell's handwriting. It was dated Sunday. He slipped it in his pocket. Jones stopped, said, 'Nothing here, I'd say.'

'Nothing in the safe.'

Jones slammed the safe door shut and spun the combination. They went outside. Jones said, 'If we could only find a clue—'

Ten minutes later, in his room, Parker read the letter.

Parker,

I am riding out to Watson's farm. I got a hunch something is haywire. I pack $2,000 to give him for a mortgage. This thing is closing in and hell will pop soon. I've seen that before. So just as a precaution, I'm leaving you this note to find if something happens to me. Notify Washington, collect.

Trundell.

CHAPTER TWENTY-ONE

Parker did not get a wire to the railhead. He had the solution in his hands now.

He had a .45 and belt and he put this on, tying the gun-holster down. He checked the gun and went downstairs and came to the Elkhorn Café. Millie was counting dimes and quarters, and she looked up and smiled lazily. Parker liked her slow smile and her eyes behind it.

'I'm leaving town soon,' he said.

She thought he was joking. 'Then you won't marry me?'

'I am leaving,' he assured her.

She said, 'Oh,' and then, 'Well, we'll miss you.'

'I'll see you again,' he said. 'I'll see you before I go.'

She looked out the window. 'A gambler is always on the move, isn't he? I couldn't ever be a gambler, or his wife. I like to stay in one place and put my roots deep into the soil. Look at this town. I know almost every person in it, and I know their weakness and strengths. I like that.'

'Some people do.'

'Connie Savage would make a gambler a good wife. She likes to drift like a tumbleweed in the wind.'

'Not for me,' said Parker.

He ate and went outside. Jetta Savage came out of the Fiddlefoot. She said, 'Hello, Mamma's boy,' and her smile was brittle. Kirt Stanton sat his horse across the street and watched them talk. Parker glanced at him and the range boss lifted his hand a little from the fork of his saddle. Parker nodded and returned his gaze to Jetta.

'I'm leaving the basin,' he said. 'I might ride by and say good-bye to you this evening. Will you be home?'

'Yes.'

The gambler went to his hotel room and sat and looked out the window. Sheriff Ed Jones rode out, going into the hills. Jetta Savage and Stanton loped out and headed west, running toward the buttes north of the Heart Bar Six ranch-house. Evidently they had come into town for cigarettes or tobacco and were heading out to work cattle again.

Parker got his horse and led him behind the hotel. He took down his saddlebags and warbag and paid for his hotel room. He walked over to the Double Diamond and told the proprietor he was leaving for the Little Rockies and the gold camps there. The man had seen gamblers come and go and he merely nodded.

Parker went west. An hour later he was behind the Heart Bar Six Ranch. He left his horse and went unseen to the house. The back door was open and he entered. He did not knock on Ike Savage's room, but opened the door and went inside. Savage lay with both hands on the covers, and his eyes were closed. Parker stood there for a full minute and watched the man. Savage opened his eyes and looked up.

Parker said, 'Where are your lupines?'

'The season has passed. The flowers are dead. I outlived them, Parker.' He closed his eyes. 'I loved them, too.'

'You'll have more next year.'

The eyes stayed closed, the eyelids thin and transparent.

'I heard you come,' said Savage slowly. 'I knew your step. So I just kept on with my eyes closed. You won't come much longer, I guess.'

'Why?'

'Your type rushes things through. On the surface, they look easygoing and slow, but underneath they stir things up, and they rush them to a conclusion. You've been here some days. Now you'll go.'

'You see much,' murmured Parker.

'I've seen too much.'

Parker said, 'You're right. This is the last time I'll see you, Mr. Savage. I am through here, almost. There are just a few long strings to pull to close the sack. It won't be pretty.'

'My daughters?'

Parker fabricated, 'Your daughters are

161

clean of this; they do not tie into it. I thought perhaps they would be a string or two in this tangle, but they came out without being involved. You may rest assured of that, sir. Your daughters might drink and run around, but they are clean of all this.'

A short silence. Then: 'I'd like to believe you, sir.'

'You have your choice, Mr. Savage.'

The eyelids lifted. 'I believe you, sir.'

'Then I'll leave you, Mr. Savage.'

One hand lifted, forefinger extended, then dropped. 'There are a few questions. Why did Mack try to kill you outside when you were here last?'

'Mack was part of the gang,' said Parker. 'He had instructions from up above to kill me. But luck was with me and I got him instead.'

'And Crazy Springs?'

Parker told him quietly, 'The Indian was involved in it, too. He got in too deep for his own comfort; he wanted to talk to me. When he met me on the range, he got afraid and pulled back. Then he came to my room to see me. One of them knifed him to keep him silent.'

'Who knifed him?'

'I do not want to tell. But I know the man now.'

'Who killed Luke Smith?'

'I have my suspicions, but I am not dead

162

sure. By tonight, I will be. You may be assured that when, and if, I ride out of Muleshoe Basin, the man who killed Luke Smith will be in jail, or dead.'

Savage let the silence grow. Parker thought he had gone to sleep and he took one long last look at the shrivelled face. But Savage spoke again. 'I like you, sir. Your money—your fifty thousand—awaits you in the bank. I wish you good luck.'

'It's still your money,' said Parker.

'You do not want it?'

'No.'

'That's a lot of money.'

Parker said, 'I've won that and more in an hour, in a minute. Money does me no good. It comes and goes. I have no respect for money. If I had, I could have thousands of dollars stored away in various banks for bankers to get rich on. That money is yours, and you keep it.'

'Connie will get it.'

'Let her get it. Let her buy whisky with it. That will of yours caused some of this. But you know that now.'

'Let them fight,' said Ike Savage. 'Let them fight. Then they can't fight with me.' He closed his eyes, and Parker left.

The gambler walked down the hall. He went out openly and went around the house and stood by the corner. Chickens clucked and rolled in the pasture below the corrals.

The old mozo was cleaning the barn. The windmill squeaked a little as it lifted cold water. Parker went toward Connie's bungalow. He knocked.

'Come in.'

She wore a simple housedress. She looked long at him. 'Well, the great Mr. Parker. Out to visit Connie Savage, huh? This is a surprise.'

Parker looked around the cabin. A bed stood in the far corner, a blue spread on it, and beside it was a walnut dresser, the top covered with feminine necessities. The floor was hardwood and the windows sparkled with clean white drapes. The gambler turned his attention to the woman.

'You're a fine woman, when you're sober.'

'Maybe I drink for a purpose.'

'You tried to keep her out of it,' said Parker. 'I feel that you did, and that you failed. The will drove her wild, I guess. Then you took to drink to hide your sense of failure, of neglect. You liked the taste, you kept on.'

Connie was silent, her eyes watchful. She laughed throatily. 'Go on,' she said.

'But it didn't pay. Day by day you got further apart. Day by day she drifted in further with them. She got too deep. You were in the south that day I came in and pulled Luke Smith out of that fire. You saw me and you didn't know where I stood.'

'Where do you stand?'

'I'll tell you . . . now. This will soon be over; the fire will be ashes. I stand against you and your sister. I stand there because an old man—an old man who is dying—asked me to stand against his own flesh and blood. Trundell is dead. They've killed him to silence him. But they haven't left the country yet. I saw two of them today—the big two.'

She was sobbing.

'I don't want to hurt you, Connie; you've been hurt enough. You've hid it under a thin veneer that was applied by whiskey. Have her here tonight. Have Stanton with her. Will you do that for me?'

'Yes, I'll try.'

'Do that,' he said.

She came closer to him. She looked at him, and her eyes held tears. She said, 'Parker, kiss me.'

Her lips were moist. She clung to him, and he let her sob. Finally she wiped her eyes with a small handkerchief.

'She'll be here, Parker.'

'I'll see you before I go,' he said.

He left her and went outside into the clean quick sunshine.

He met Sheriff Ed Jones at Wishbone Creek. 'Are you looking for me?' he said.

'Yes.'

Parker looked at the sinking sun. 'I got the whole answer now,' he said. 'I want you to go with me; I want you to help me.'

Jones nodded.

CHAPTER TWENTY-TWO

They came into Watson's farm. The man was milking a cow in the corral. They opened the corral gate and Watson looked at them sharply. 'Why the visit out here?' he asked.

'That grey horse in the barn?' asked Parker. 'He's your horse, isn't he?'

'Yes.'

'The man who killed Luke Smith rode that horse,' said Parker. 'I saw that horse in the storm, but the man didn't see me. He rode that horse to make anybody believe that the sheriff here had killed Smith.'

Watson kept on milking. He had his head buried in the flank of the patient cow. His eyes were hidden. 'You talk like a fool,' he said. 'The sheriff's grey has markings on his rump. My grey hasn't.'

Parker put one boot under the milk stool and kicked. Watson slipped into the dust, the milk spilling. The cow trotted off. Watson got up, anger scrawled across his face. Parker hit him and knocked him back. Watson put up his right fist, and Parker drove through it and knocked him down.

'Now get up and be good,' said the

gambler. 'Somebody's put ink—printer's ink—on that grey's rump to make him look like Jones' bronc. You can see it on his hide. You didn't wash it off well enough.'

'You look at the horse?'

'Yes, I did.'

Watson looked at Jones. 'You don't believe that crazy story, do you Sheriff?'

Jones nodded. 'Trundell came out this way last Sunday. Nobody's seen him since. He had two thousand dollars on him. You've murdered him. We found his grave out in the hills.' That last was a fabrication, but Watson would not know that.

Watson studied him.

Parker spoke. 'You're not the main fry in this, Watson; you're small pennies. We know who the big fellows are.' He named two names.

Watson wiped blood from his mouth. 'I don't understand you,' he said.

Parker tried again. 'They're running a counterfeit ring here. You're part of it. Trundell was a government man who posed as a banker to get in and crack the ring. I myself got a ten-dollar bill—a bum one—one night across my table. I know now who gave it to me.'

Watson said, 'I don't know anything. I can't say anything because I don't know what you are talking about.'

Jones looked at Parker. 'We could make

him remember, maybe.'

Parker shook his head. 'Tie him up and we'll pick him up later.'

Watson had a rifle against the far corral. He ran for it. He had to pass Ed Jones. Jones had his short-gun out. He beefed the farmer and knocked him down and landed on him, pinning him to the corral dust.

'He's out,' he said.

Parker got a rope from the barn. Jones stayed in the corral, sitting on Watson. The cow stood and looked at them as though wondering what this was all about. Jones tied Watson hand and foot and gagged him with his bandanna. The exertion brought a coughing spell that almost doubled him. Finally he straightened and asked what they would do with the farmer.

'Roll him in the house and lock it until we get back.'

'What if he gets loose and gets away?'

'He can't get far. You can get to the railroad and get a wire out and the law will get him in a day or so. He hasn't a chance and he knows it.'

Parker helped carry the tied-up farmer into the house. They laid him on the floor and locked the door, with Jones pocketing the key. They got their horses and started south. Jones was openly worried.

'They might have got cold boots and pulled out.'

Parker said, 'I saw them both today.'

*   *   *

Day was changing to dusk. They took to the rimrock with an eye always on the bottoms below. The twilight died and darkness was slowly pushing back the light. They rode for some distance. Finally Parker said, 'This is close enough.'

They left their horses tied in the brush. They went down the slope and found the creek, and they went along this. Finally they came to a clearing. A cabin sat in it, and right behind it was a hill.

Parker said, 'You watch my back,' and he walked openly forward, heading toward the cabin.

A dog came out, barking. Behind him came a man. He looked at Parker carefully. He said, 'Hello, Parker. On foot.'

'My horse broke his leg, André.'

The humpback said, 'That's too bad.' He looked at Parker's gun. 'Why throw down on me?'

Parker stood stock-still. 'You're coming into town with me, André. The charge is murder and counterfeiting. The murder occurred when you painted that grey horse of Watson's to make him look like Jones' grey and when you killed Luke Smith.'

'Who told you this crazy story?'

Jones came out of the brush by the house. He said, 'You got him, huh?'

'See if Hawkins is around,' asked Parker.

Jones went towards the house. He went inside. André looked at Parker, a smile on his lips. 'Who told you this craziness?'

'Watson.'

André was silent.

Parker went on, building up. 'You played a wide loop, you and Hawkins. You even helped Jetta Savage and Kirt Stanton steal Heart Bar Six cattle and sell them. You ran this counterfeiting scheme pretty well. So you killed Trundell, huh? He left me a note, saying he was riding this way.'

'I don't know what you are talking about.'

'Hawkins made the big mistake,' said Parker. He was watching the man closely. 'That was when he accidentally gave me that bum ten-dollar bill in the Double Diamond. He made another mistake, too. After he knifed Crazy Springs, he just sat in the lobby, waiting for me. Maybe he wanted to kill me, too.'

Jones said, 'Hawkins ain't here,' and came out of the house.

A rifle spoke from the buckbrush. Jones went down on his knees. André hollered, 'Cover me, Hawkins!' and started running. He was pulling his gun, too.

Parker went to one knee, his six-shooter coming out. He did not shoot at André but

170

sent his lead at Hawkins in the brush. He glimpsed part of the man, and the gun spoke three times. Hawkins came out of the brush. Parker shot twice more, shot squarely. He sent his last bullet home. 'That's for Trundell,' he said.

He turned, gun empty. André was down, too. Sheriff Jones was walking toward him, gun in hand, limping a little. 'Got me in the leg,' he said slowly. 'I got André; he's alive, I guess.'

Parker's knees were wooden. He went down beside the man. 'He's alive like fun,' he said.

'What about Hawkins?'

'He's dead,' Parker said, 'I know that.'

Jones said slowly, 'My leg—it hurts.' He hobbled into the cabin, coughing as he walked. Parker got a knife and slit his pants and the wound lay in his thigh. He got a towel and bound it after he had washed it out with turpentine from a bottle by the door. Tears of pain rolled from Jones' eyes as the turpentine bit.

'What will we do with them?'

Parker considered. 'You will ride into town. Get help and get Watson. Better notify Washington about Trundell, too. Watson'll have something to say on that, I suppose. He might get off easier at the trial.'

'And you?'

'Then get men out here to look this place

over,' said Parker.

Jones repeated, 'And you?'

'You get your horse and go,' said Parker. He went up on the ridge and came back leading Jones' horse. He helped Jones up.

'Damn it,' growled Jones. 'I asked about you?'

'I'll look around for a while. Then I'll go west to the Little Rockies. I'm through here.'

Jones said, 'So long,' and rode off.

★   ★   ★

Parker went back into the house. He tapped the floor and pounded it and found the cellar. He went down it and through a shaft and he came to a cave. There was a lamp lit in it. He looked at the painting for some time. He looked the place over carefully.

He went back down the tunnel and into the house. He got his horse and rode out. Behind him André and Hawkins lay limp on the grass. Two hours later he rode into the Heart Bar Six. He rode right up to Connie's cabin. He stepped down and let his horse trail his reins.

'Miss Connie?'

The door opened and showed her. 'Come in,' she said.

Parker went inside. Kirt Stanton stood against the wall, looking at him coldly. The gambler nodded to him. Jetta sat on the bed, her smile brittle. 'Hello,' she said.

'You're not so gay,' said Parker.

Jetta was silent. Stanton spoke. 'Don't rub it in, gambler. You got the top hand. Connie's told us. What happened?'

'Where do you stand in this?'

Stanton looked at Jetta. 'We ran off Heart Bar Six cattle. Hawkins and André helped us. We got a good sum in a bank in Great Falls. They got their cut.'

'The counterfeiting?'

'Not in on that,' said Stanton.

Parker looked at Jetta. 'That right?'

She nodded.

Parker said, 'Give her a drink; she needs it.' Connie handed her a bottle. Jetta raised it to drink and Parker smashed it to the floor. The pint rolled over and the liquor jetted out. Jetta looked at it.

She raised her eyes. 'Well?'

'André is dead,' said Parker. 'So is Jed Hawkins. Hawkins worked it slick, trying to get into my confidence. Jones knows all about it. Right now, Jones is riding into town, filled with this news. Watson is in jail by now. He might talk; he might implicate you two.'

Connie looked slowly at Parker.

Stanton was looking at Jetta. Jetta said, 'We'll stand it, gambler. We'll go to court and—'

Parker jerked a thumb toward the house. 'And break that old man's heart? You'd drag

173

him through the mud again? You've done enough to him, both of you. You won't take his name into a dirty court scandal!'

Stanton asked, 'Well, then what can we do?'

'Jones knows about your share. We have talked it over. He hates Ike Savage; but he loves a fighter. We've made a plan.'

Jetta smiled crookedly. 'Oh, yes!'

'What is it?' asked Stanton.

Parker spoke to the man directly. 'Take her away, Stanton. Take her away from Montana, out of the state. Go any place. Will you do that?'

Stanton looked at Jetta. 'If she is willing.'

Connie was silent. Parker was silent. Stanton was silent. Jetta said, 'All right. We'll go.'

Parker released his breath. 'That's good,' he said.

He went outside. He left the three of them there in that cabin. The night air was strong and clean and good. He got on his horse and rode toward Elkhorn. He saw a light in Ike Savage's window.

Soon Ike Savage would be dead. Ground would enfold him and work on him and take him back into its own. He believed the word of a gambler. He believed that his daughters had not been in on this. Far better to believe that than to die with their treachery on his mind, eating like acid.

174

Parker rode into the night. He would go through Elkhorn on his way to Wood Mountain in Canada. He was thinking of Millie Williams. He would see her before he went to Canada.

Photoset, printed and bound in Great Britain by REDWOOD BURN LIMITED, Trowbridge, Wiltshire